"Come, Brianna, let me tempt you," Cane said.

He used his free hand to heap a corn chip with a moist mound of guacamole and hold it poised before her mouth. "Open, wary little wild bird," he ordered softly. "Learn to eat from my hand."

"Aren't you afraid that I might be prone to bite the hand that feeds me?" Bree responded tartly.

"Then you'd have to kiss it and make it well," was his swift topper to her cliché. "I'll take that chance any day. Bite away," he challenged deliberately.

It wasn't a game Bree had bothered to play before, but her instincts were all in excellent working order. With the softest and most careful of touches she took the chip into her mouth, then with a quick, sideways movement of her head, she nipped his forefinger. After calmly swallowing the chip Cane had fed her, Bree informed him sweetly, "It's sometimes dangerous to dare a Graeme. We're not noted for stepping back from a challenge. Now shall I kiss it and make it well?"

"I suppose I can spare one finger," he allowed doubtfully, holding his hand out to Bree. . . .

WHAT ARE *LOVESWEPT* ROMANCES?

They are stories of true romance and touching emotion. We believe those two very important ingredients are constants in our highly sensual and very believable stories in the *LOVESWEPT* line. Our goal is to give you, the reader, stories of consistently high quality that may sometimes make you laugh, sometimes make you cry, but are always fresh and creative and contain many delightful surprises within their pages.

Most romance fans read an enormous number of books. Those they truly love, they keep. Others may be traded with friends and soon forgotten. We hope that each *LOVESWEPT* romance will be a treasure—a "keeper." We will always try to publish

LOVE STORIES YOU'LL NEVER FORGET
BY AUTHORS YOU'LL ALWAYS REMEMBER

The Editors

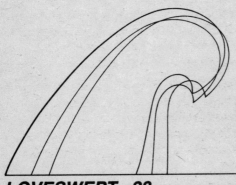

LOVESWEPT • 28

Anne N. Reisser
Love, Catch A Wild Bird

 BANTAM BOOKS • TORONTO • NEW YORK • LONDON • SYDNEY

LOVE, CATCH A WILD BIRD
A Bantam Book / January 1984

LOVESWEPT and the wave device are trademarks of
Bantam Books, Inc.

ISBN 0-553-21637-6

Published simultaneously in the United States and Canada

Bantam Books are published by Bantam Books, Inc. Its
trademark, consisting of the words "Bantam Books" and the
portrayal of a rooster, is Registered in U.S. Patent and Trademark Office and in other countries. Marca Registrada. Bantam
Books, Inc., 666 Fifth Avenue, New York, New York 10103.

PRINTED IN THE UNITED STATES OF AMERICA

O   0 9 8 7 6 5 4 3 2 1

One

"Yowee! Bree's coming home! Bree's coming home!"

The jubilant shout penetrated even the profound absorption of the two men. They had been bent, in earnest conversation, above the hub of the futuristically tapered blades of a windmill rotor which was supported by sturdy, strategically placed wooden sawhorses. The taller of the two men straightened gingerly, absentmindedly massaging his spine at the back of his waist while cocking his head in a listening attitude. A slow, easy smile lifted the corners of his mouth.

"Sounds as though Drew's really excited about something. You got an oil well that was due to come a gusher?" The amused drawl echoed the humorous gleam warming deep-set, dark blue eyes.

His companion chuckled. "Don't I wish!" he replied ruefully. "But, if I heard him correctly, he was announcing something just as explosive as a new gusher. He did yell 'Bree's coming home!' didn't he?"

"That's what it sounded like to me," the lazy drawl affirmed.

Before either man could continue, a teenage whirlwind burst through the door of the barnlike building and thudded across the concrete floor. Echoes of his boisterous progress reverberated around the metal rafters, bouncing hollowly off the underside of the corrugated roof of the high-ceilinged structure.

"Alex! Cane! Bree's coming home!" The beaming smile that stretched Drew's wide mouth amply indicated his delight in the news he was imparting. "Mom said she just called. She's finished her latest project and she's on her way home. Isn't that just super?" He sucked in a necessary breath and continued in a rattle of words. "She hurt her ribs during that last rafting trip and she's coming home to recuperate before she starts another project."

"Hurt her ribs! Is she all right?" Alex's quick concern made the anxious question crack sharply in the echoing cavern.

"Of course she is," his brother assured him cheerfully, with the confidence of carefree youth. "You know Bree. Why, she told Mom that she's driving the Blazer by herself, and pulling the trailer too, so she can't have busted herself up *too* badly."

"Andrew Graeme, you callous young devil . . ." His exasperated older brother said as he swiped widely at the grinning young boy. Drew merely danced nimbly out of reach with the ease of long and frequent practice.

"Aw, Alex, you know that Bree's practically indestructible," Drew said, defending his seemingly casual attitude.

"It's the 'practically' that worries me," Alex muttered darkly.

Drew ignored that poor spirited comment and continued proudly, "Bree'll take something as simple as a few cracked ribs without even breaking stride. Why, remember the time she broke her arm, while she was bronc riding in the amateur rodeo? A week later she wrapped a plastic bag around her cast and went water skiing. Bree doesn't slow down for anything." Admiration and wistful excitement flickered across his thin young face. "Even if she's not really hurt, I hope she'll stay around for a while. Bree's so much *fun.* Things happen when she's at home. Besides, Mom's awfully excited. You know how much she misses Bree and . . . and I think she sort of worries about her when she's gone."

"We all worry about her," Alex rejoined grimly. "Does Dad know she's on her way home?"

"Not yet. Do you know where he is? He wasn't in any of the barns so I thought he might be down here with you and Cane." Drew fidgeted restlessly, obviously eager to find his father. "Mom promised that I could tell him about Bree and I'm also supposed to remind him to call Dan McAllen about that young bull. Mom said that Mr. McAllen called to say that he's had another offer on the bull, but that Dad still has the right of first refusal."

Alex grinned slightly, amused by Drew's obvious determination to preserve his chosen role as the bearer of happy tidings. "Dad and Carlos drove off in the pickup about an hour and a half ago," he said. "I think they were going into town to get the new fencing. He should be back any time now, but I imagine that he and Carlos will go directly to the south pasture, where the fence went down. Why don't you throw a saddle over that cross-eyed mule of yours and see if you can catch up with Dad there?"

"Don't you call Beelzebub a mule!" Drew sputtered heatedly in defense of his beloved horse. "Just because he bit you the last time you were shoeing him is no reason to insult him. If it weren't for the fact that you and I share the same parents, I'd tell you that his bloodlines are a darn sight better than *yours*!"

But Drew was too excited to stay and exchange further friendly insults with his brother. He could do that any time. The chance to announce Bree's imminent homecoming was an event rare enough to take priority over almost any other activity. He whirled himself away as quickly as he had whirled himself in.

"Whew! He makes me feel ancient," Cane said wryly as the door banged shut behind the fast moving boy.

"Not so much of that, if you please," Alex laughed. "You're less than a year older than I am. If you *really* want to feel decrepit, just wait until you meet Bree. Then the gray hairs will start to sprout like weeds in an unsprayed grain field. I guarantee it!"

"Who's Bree? I've gathered that she's female and formidable and *very* welcome, not to mention probably exhausting, but . . ." Cane's voice trailed away invitingly.

"There's no probably about it." Alex grimaced. "She *is* exhausting. She's my sister, Brianna Elizabeth Graeme, Bree to everyone who knows and loves her, which is a wholly redundant phrase, as you'll discover as soon as you meet her. If you think that *Drew* is full of energy, well, 'you ain't seen nuthin' yet!' Bree could generate as many watts as a whole bank of these rotors without even raising a sweat and still have energy left over."

"Mmmm?" Cane responded encouragingly, as the two men bent over their task again. "She doesn't work on the ranch, then? I don't think I would have overlooked someone that . . . ah . . . exuberant, even in the short time I've been here."

"No, you wouldn't have been able to overlook Bree," Alex agreed with a strangely anticipatory grin. He certainly planned to be somewhere in the vicinity to observe Cane's first exposure to his sister. "Bree's always been the one with the wanderlust in this generation of our family. There seems to be at least one in each generation of Graemes. My father's brother, Ben, for instance, was one who had it. And Bree's got the full dose for this generation, I'm afraid. Neither Drew nor I seem to want to wander farther than to town on Saturday night. But Bree, well," he gestured expressively with his free hand, "she always had the urge to see what was on the other side of the mountain. From the time she could crawl, she was harder to keep corralled than a basket full of frogs, and she's still as independent as a hog on ice."

He sighed heavily. "Most older brothers are supposed to resent having a younger sister trail around behind them, but let me tell you, that's a hell of a lot easier than having to spend your time trying to *catch up* with your younger sister!

"Bree," he mourned, "does not automatically

recognize the natural superiority of either my advanced age or my sex. She's four years younger and half a foot shorter, but do you think that impresses her? Not likely! Not that she *competes* with me, you understand," Alex added with careful emphasis. "*I* have more respect for the continued integrity of my skin than to subject it to Bree's idea of fun."

"Rather a bit of a daredevil, I gather," Cane concluded in a thoughtful voice, but Alex noticed that he didn't smile indulgently when he said it, as so many people were prone to do when Bree's penchant for dangerous pastimes was discussed.

Bree's family didn't smile either. With varying degrees of fatalistic dread, they chewed their nails and waited for the phone to ring when she was off on one of her projects, but they loved her dearly and rejoiced wholeheartedly at each safe homecoming. Bree was . . . Bree. One loved her, laughed with her, and let her go with a smile, a hug, and a kiss when the thirst for new skies overcame her, as it always did.

"Drew mentioned that your sister was coming home to recuperate," Cane probed, encouraging Alex to continue with his flow of information. This Bree sounded like quite an interesting character.

"Oh Lord, yes." Alex groaned, sudden creases of worry furrowing his tanned forehead. "Drew's convinced that Bree is indestructible," he said, excusing his younger brother's seeming lack of concern. "And I'm glad to admit that she has led a charmed life thus far, but some day she's going to dream up a project that she might not be able to walk away from." Cane looked appropriately puzzled and Alex obligingly explained. "Bree's a freelance writer. She's discovered the perfect way to make her enthusiasm for adventure pay off. Handsomely." Alex's admission held an undertone of grudging respect and wry resignation. "She writes about her escapades—she calls them projects—and son-of-a-gun if there isn't a real market for her stories. Magazines *ask* her to do feature articles for them and they *pay* for them."

Pride and bewilderment were amusingly mingled in his expression. "Newspaper articles, pieces for the Sunday supplements, you name it: my mother has compiled a collection of Bree's stuff that has already filled three scrapbooks." He grinned. "I'll warn you right now that Mom will spread a scrapbook in your lap without any prompting at all, given the slightest opening, which generally occurs during the first time you're invited for dinner. But it really isn't such an awful price to pay for some darned good cooking," he hastened to reassure Cane. "Bree's a talented writer and she has a real gift for description." He brooded for a moment. "It's just that sometimes it's a damned uncomfortable gift when you happen to remember that it was *your* sister who was hand feeding those orcas and playing tag with a bunch of blasted manta rays!"

"I'd enjoy reading her articles sometime," Cane said, and he wasn't just being polite. He liked the Graemes. They were friendly, hard working, and as a family, openly affectionate and closely knit, everything his own family was—whenever they were able to gather, from their various far-flung careers, at his parents' retirement home in Florida. He was a stranger in the Graemes' midst, here to do a job. Still it was a pleasure to observe, even from the outside, a family unit which hadn't lost its loving solidarity. Besides, even making allowances for a perfectly understandable family bias, the woman probably could write an interesting story if she was able to support herself with the proceeds from her pen. Or typewriter.

The afternoon sun had lost none of its strength by the time Cane and the senior Graeme, Adam, finished their conference and walked out of the shelter of the sprawling ranch house. By unspoken, mutual consent they paused briefly beneath the shade of the redwood beamed porch, absorbing and adjusting to the impact of the thick, hot air on lungs acclimated for the past hour to the thin, artificial chill of air conditioning. The bulk of the house at their backs protected them from the persistent wind. It streamed ceaselessly over the acres of the ranch on its way inland, through a funnel of hills from the cooler California coastal lands, into the dry and sweltering interior valleys.

Cane watched the brisk wind comb its rough fingers through the dry, golden grass carpeting hills that rose on all sides above the narrow green oasis that girdled the main ranch house. His knowledgeable eyes assessed the wind's potential with satisfaction. Three generations of Graemes had farmed their acres with crops and cattle. With his help, they could add another crop. His job was to enable them to farm the wind.

"The concrete of the pads has cured, Adam," Cane said, continuing his conversation with the graying, burly rancher who stood silently at his side, "and we're ready to erect the first two towers. Alex and I have started balancing the first rotors and I've got a crew coming tomorrow to start on the towers. We'll also be ready to start pouring more pads by the end of the week. I've had confirmation on the shipment of the components of the next three turbines. Everything else is back on schedule and the transmission lines will be strung in plenty of time before the first turbine is ready to start generating."

The calm confidence in Cane's words and voice was an integral part of his personality. The grizzled rancher standing at his side had already been a pleased witness to this quiet competence, for Cane had untangled the snarled schedule created by the bankruptcy of the first company that had tried, and failed, to set up an efficient, producing windfarm on his wind-scoured acres. After the first company had sunk rapidly and ingloriously beneath a sea of red ink, Cane and his partners had approached the Graemes with a well-capitalized, carefully researched proposal.

"Alex told me that things were moving along pretty smoothly," Adam admitted.

"Alex has been a big help," Cane said. "He's good with his hands and he has a real feel for machinery."

Adam grinned. "A rancher has a number of rules he has to live by if he hopes to survive in today's economy, and one of the most stringent is: Don't buy a new anything. Know how to fix the old anything. Besides, since we've now bought a piece of your action, Alex and I decided that at least one of us ought to learn about this new generation of windmills, from the ground up, if you'll pardon the pun."

"As a limited partner, you're allowed a limited pun," Cane replied with his characteristic slow grin, "but to tell you the truth, we're all learning about the new wind power technology from the ground up. We have to pull together a lot of different disciplines, including meteorology, electrical and aeronautical engineering, as well as construction engineering, my own field."

Cane was speaking, but his attention was no longer fully focused on his companion. Eyes narrowed, he watched a plume of dust rise where he knew the road to the ranch ran, although the road itself, and whatever traveled on it, was hidden behind the shoulder of a gentle hill. "Company's coming," he murmured, directing Adam's attention toward the telltale cloud.

The older man sucked in his breath sharply. "I hope it's not just 'company,'" he said soberly. "My daughter is due to arrive sometime today. She's been gone for some months and we'll all be very glad to have her home again." The simple words were poignant.

"I was with Alex when Drew gave his imitation of Paul Revere a couple of days ago," Cane said, deliberately lightening the atmosphere, which, for a moment, had vibrated with all of Adam's unexpressed concern for his daughter's safety.

Adam relaxed abruptly and laughed. "We all tend to get excited when Bree's on her way home," he agreed with a broad grin. "Mary has been baking ever since she hung up the phone. Say"—a thought seemed to strike him happily—"why don't you plan to have dinner with us tonight? I can guarantee some good food, and plenty of it."

In normal circumstances Cane would have been loath to intrude on a private family celebration, but this time curiosity made him hesitate before answering. He had no chance, however, to either accept or reject the invitation, because Adam leaned forward suddenly, his calloused hands gripping the porch railing as he stared intently at the vehicles that had suddenly come into view where the road curved around in front of the hill.

"It's Bree!" her excited father exclaimed joyously. He whirled and with two long strides reached the door to the house. He yanked it open and yelled, "Mary, Bree's here! Bree's come home!"

As though those words were a cue in a play, activity began to erupt from all sides with startling rapidity. Adam barely had time to step back from the open door, still holding it wide, before his wife catapulted past him, across the porch and out into the front yard, where she paused, shading her eyes with an upflung hand as she stared eagerly toward the road. Adam hastily joined her and threw an arm around her shoulders, waiting with her to welcome their daughter home.

Cane walked over and quietly closed the door Adam had forgotten to shut. As he turned back toward the front yard, several more flashes of motion caught his attention. From the left, Alex came running up from the barn with long, loping strides. From the right, pacing the small caravan—for now Cane could see that what he had first thought were two cars was in reality a four-wheel-drive vehicle pulling a trailer—Drew, on the much maligned Beelzebub, raced in a noisy escort, whooping a shrill welcome. Three dogs, their plumy tails waving like frenzied metronomes, appeared to add their full throated approval and greeting to the pandemonium of the prodigal's return.

The mud-splattered, dust-filmed, green and white Blazer, towing the only slightly less travel-stained trailer, steered carefully down the track to the house, spitting dust and gravel from beneath the deep treaded tires. As the entourage drew to a halt, Drew sheared away to one side, threw himself from the saddle of his nervously dancing horse and raced forward, still whooping exuberantly. Beelzebub, ears laid flat and tail held high, took that opportunity to race away toward the sanctuary of his quiet stall in the barn. Cane alone noted his precipitate departure.

As the door of the Blazer opened, humans and dogs converged. Cane caught only the briefest glimpse of a laughing face and a dark, curly head before the occupant of the Blazer was engulfed by her jubilant welcoming committee. For some minutes thereafter, his only view was a kaleidoscope of surging backs and wildly waving arms.

At last the cheerful tumult subsided to the point that individual voices could be distinguished. "Alex, you and Andrew get your sister's clothes out of the trailer and bring in the perishables from the refrigerator. And bring in her plants too. It'll be too hot for them to stay in that closed-up trailer. When that's done, Alex can take the trailer around back and unhook it. Bree, a hot shower and a cold drink are what you can expect inside." Mary Graeme's efficient generalship received obedient "Yes ma'am's!" from her sons and as they moved away to begin their appointed tasks, Cane had his first, unimpeded view of Brianna.

Two

Brianna grimaced slightly when she reached around behind herself to pull the sweaty knit shirt away from the small of her back, where it clung damply. Her ribs might not actually be broken, but the muscles she had wrenched and bruised were reminding her that she hadn't gotten off scot-free by any means. It had been an incredibly asinine, but unfortunately instinctive, action on her part, she admitted with silent disgust—and not for the first time since she had gone over the side of the boat to rescue the drowning dog. It wasn't much comfort to her aching side to remind herself that the real fool in the fiasco had been the doting idiot of a woman who had brought the yapping Poopsie along with her on the trip, not to mention the guide who had let his appreciation of Poopsie's Momsie's cleavage—so generously displayed!—sway his judgment and allow the dog into the raft in the first place. And the wretched beast had even had the nerve to bite her while she was saving it from a watery death! "*How sharper than a serpent's tooth is an ungrateful poodle,*" she misquoted silently.

Her mother's suggestion of a shower and a cold drink was the best offer she'd had in the last two hundred fifty miles. The trailer had all the comforts of home, of course, but the shower stall was undeniably close quarters. It would be nice to take a shower without the omnipresent threat of finally succumbing to claustrophobia. When sweat began to trickle down from the beads that had formed at her hairline, rolling past her ears in small drops, she decided that the cold drink her mother had mentioned would also rate high on her list of desirable home amenities, ranking right up there next to the efficient air conditioning her parents had had installed when they had built the new ranch house. Flanked by her mother and her father, she headed toward the house.

As she passed from the bright sunlight of the open yard into the relative dimness of the shaded porch, a tall shadow stepped forward and politely opened the front door for her. She blinked, trying to accelerate the adjustment her pupils were making from sunlight to shade, but succeeded only in giving herself the quaintly endearing, wide-eyed appearance of a small, delightfully inquiring owl. Her involuntarily breathed "Who? . . ." might have extended the simile to ridiculous lengths except that Brianna's eyes had finally completed their adjustment to the dimmer light. She saw Cane's face clearly for the first time. Her involuntary "Who?" was immediately followed by an equally involuntary smile of such spontaneous warmth that all of Cane's thoughts of teasing analogies skittered away like water droplets on a hot griddle. No owl had ever possessed a smile like Brianna's!

She held out her hand and said softly, "Hello. I'm Brianna Graeme." The catch and depth in her voice could have been attributed to the travel dryness of her throat.

Cane clasped her hand between his large ones, cradling it in the most careful of grips, as he responded, "Hello, Brianna Graeme. I'm Cane Taylor." His voice was also deeply husky, but he'd finished a cold, wet beer with Adam not more than thirty minutes before.

"Are you staying for supper, Cane?" Brianna's words might have been taken for a polite question. Her smile made it an irresistible invitation.

"I would like very much to stay for supper," Cane said firmly.

Brianna didn't look away from Cane. "Mother, Cane is staying for supper," she announced abstractedly.

"We're glad to have him, Bree," Mary murmured.

No one moved. Cane still held Brianna's hand in that careful grip and she showed no immediate desire to reclaim it. They might have played statues for an indefinite time had not the world, in the persons of Alex and Drew, intruded noisily.

"Hey! What's the hold-up? Bree, if you don't hurry and get a move on, your plants are going to get a bad sunburn," Alex jested, peering around from behind the small forest of greenery he clutched precariously in his arms. He halted outside the shade of the front porch, waiting impatiently for his kin to clear away from the front door. "Ow!" Drew, his vision impaired by the pile of clothes he was carrying, had run up on Alex's heels, stabbing his brother in the back with the hook of a clothes-hanger.

A shrill yelp echoed Alex's pained ejaculation. Drew, trying to maintain his balance after colliding with Alex's hard frame, had stepped backward onto one of the dogs' feet. The aggrieved animal, knowing better than to vent his just outrage on the author of his injury, had in turn snapped reflexively at his nearby canine companion and, more by ill luck than good management, had nipped the tender skin of the other dog's ear. A full-fledged, noisy canine brawl promptly followed.

Alex cursed roundly and colorfully while he rid himself of Bree's flora, cracking several painted clay pots in the process. Adam yelled for Drew to keep away from the battling dogs and when Alex's hands were free, Adam and his older son waded into the fray. With experienced dispatch they separated the combatants, dragging them apart by their collars and the scruffs of their necks. Then with stern commands, they quelled the snarling bundles of fury.

When some semblance of calm had finally been restored, Alex walked back to the porch to take up his burden of ferns and flowers. Brianna, to her discredit, had been unable to restrain her sense of humor and had been leaning against the door-jamb chortling at the chain of disasters. She subdued her unseemly—and unappreciated—mirth and asked with sincere concern, "You and Dad didn't get bitten, did you, Alex?"

"No, we're all right and the dogs are too, although *they* don't deserve to be," Alex grumbled. Then, with a grin and a chiding chuckle, he teased his sister. "At least I know you're really home now, Bree." And to Cane he said, "Didn't I tell you that Bree was a sure-fire formula for instant gray hairs?"

"Hey!" she objected indignantly. "I was the most innocent of bystanders."

"Bystander is right!" her brother retorted crisply, neatly reminding her that it was her hesitation at the door that had begun the whole sequence of calamity. "Let's get this show on the road, and off the front porch, before a herd of wild bulls decides to come rampaging across the front yard."

"I think that's an excellent suggestion," Adam seconded firmly. He had paused to relieve his younger son of some of the burden of clothes so that Drew could at least see where he was going. "I don't know about the rest of you," Adam rumbled as he wiped a sweaty hand across his forehead, "but *I* deserve another cold beer." He cocked his head in an exaggerated pose of listening. "Bree, quit blocking that door. I believe I hear a faint rumble of hooves."

Brianna laughed and said with unmistakable sincerity, "It's *wonderful* to be home." Her eyes swept around the loving, welcoming faces of her family and then met Cane's blue gaze once more for a long moment before she obediently entered the house.

After she had gone to her bedroom to toss her purse on the bed, Brianna joined her mother in the kitchen. She had decided that the shower would have to wait. A cold drink—and conversation—had just moved to the top of her priority list. While her mother was busy taking a number of frost-coated, heavy glass steins from a rack in the standing freezer, she ran some cold water from the tap and splashed it over her face and forearms, refreshing her travel-dusted skin.

By the time Brianna had patted her face dry on a clean dishcloth, Mary had filled two of the steins with ice cubes and now she paused to ask, "What do you want to drink, Bree, beer or a soft drink? Drew's drinking orange soda and I'm having a diet cola. The men are having beer."

"I'll have a beer," Brianna decided. "I've been drinking cola all day. What can I do to help?"

"You can get four beers and the soft drinks from the refrigerator while I get out the trays and the napkins," her mother directed briskly.

Brianna walked over to the refrigerator, opened the door and started pulling out cans, setting them on the counter next to the refrigerator. Carefully casual, she asked over her shoulder, "Who is that man?" Her pretense of mild curiosity *might* fool her mother . . . but she doubted it!

It didn't.

"Why, he told you his name, Bree dear," her mother responded with mock innocence, teasing amusement lilting beneath each word. "You don't usually have any trouble with introductions. His name is Cane Taylor."

Brianna didn't look around. She knew that her mother would be smiling broadly.

"While you're at it," Mary continued blandly, "would you get out that bowl of guacamole, please? I've got corn chips to serve with it and we'll open a can of those Spanish peanuts that your father likes so much. They'll go well with the beer, don't you think?"

"Oh, undoubtedly," Brianna agreed with a self-mocking grin as she lifted the bowl of guacamole and the fourth can of beer from the refrigerator and closed the door with a shove of her hip. Why waste time and energy trying to fool her mother? And besides, she wasn't ashamed of her interest in the man, for heaven's sake!

"I know his name," she admitted in cheerful surrender. "Now, Mother dear, tell me about Cane Taylor."

"Well," her mother began obligingly, "he isn't married, or engaged for that matter, as far as Alex has discovered. And, of lesser importance to you I'm sure, he's a partner in the company that's developing the windfarm. Cane's company took over after Mr. Bodine's company went bankrupt. Your father and Alex were so impressed by Cane's proposal that they've even invested as limited partners. Cane is here to supervise the construction. He has an apartment in town, but he's out here almost every day." She paused thoughtfully, tapping a finger against her lips. "Mmmm. That pretty well covers the essentials, I believe. If there's anything else you need or want to know about him, I'm sure that you're more than capable of discovering it for yourself."

"I always did say that the research is the most enjoyable part of any project," Brianna agreed demurely, but a wicked mischief sparkled in the depths of her green eyes.

Her expression assumed an even more suspiciously sober aspect. "I would like to take this opportunity to congratulate you, Mother, on your concise yet comprehensive briefing technique. You have just demonstrated an admirable talent for conveying the maximum amount of usable information with a minimum of verbiage." Brianna didn't dare look over at her mother. Let her top that if she could!

She could. Mary had never been slow on the comeback. "And you, my dearest daughter, are demonstrating an unsuspected but deplorable talent for paralyzing," Mary intoned, straightfaced, while she poured the beer into the frosted mugs and arranged them evenly on a round lacquered tray. "I sincerely hope that you haven't taken to writing your articles in words of ten syllables or more. Your publishers will be forced to issue a dictionary with each article!"

Undaunted, Brianna said, "Now *there's* an advertising gimmick! And it's clear that I got both my flowing eloquence *and* my vocabulary from your side of the family."

"Your erudition is exceeded only by your modesty," her mother riposted.

"You only say that because it's true," Brianna rejoined rather feebly, gallant to the last.

Honor satisfied, they holstered their thesauruses and finished loading the trays. That done, Mary deliberately appropriated the much heavier one, serenely ignoring Brianna's protest and vehement assurance that she wasn't "an invalid, for Pete's sake!"

"I don't know any Pete," her mother retorted, "and besides, I saw you wince when Drew forgot and hugged you too hard. You might not have succeeded in actually cracking your ribs this time"— Mary threw a sternly disapproving look at her unrepentant daughter—"but you're still pretty sore, and don't try to tell me otherwise, Brianna Elizabeth Graeme. Also I've carried heavier loads than this tray full of drinks before, including *you* as a toddler."

Brianna subsided more or less meekly, realizing that rank had indisputably been pulled on her. She picked up her assigned tray, which bore only the bowl of bright green guacamole, the wicker baskets heaped with crisp corn chips and two small pottery bowls of red-skinned Spanish peanuts. A wise Graeme didn't argue with "Mom" when she changed into "Mother," especially when she used one's full name. One merely jumped and then asked "how high?" on the way up.

Brianna followed her mother into the family room where her father and Cane Taylor sat talking, waiting for the women to join them. The men broke off their conversation and rose to their feet when the two women entered the room. With an instinct as natural and as automatic as breathing, Brianna's eyes sought Cane's and discovered that he was looking at her, moving toward her, hands outstretched. He lifted the tray out of her hands and then smiled down at her with a light challenge, as though daring her to object.

"You shouldn't be carrying heavy trays," he chided gently, but the soft concern in his tone and the warm smile in his blue eyes robbed the words of any possible critical impact. "Drew told me that you'd cracked some ribs in an accident."

Brianna grinned ruefully. "Knowing Drew's fondness for the dramatic, I can imagine that everyone must have been expecting me to arrive encased in plaster from head to heel, but the truth, while painful, is quite a bit tamer. No cracked ribs, just some pulled muscles and technicolor bruises. And," she nodded her head toward her mother's tray and then indicated the lightly burdened one he still held balanced easily in his big hands, "carrying a tray was hardly likely to do permanent damage. I will admit that I'm not up to heaving feed sacks around with much abandon, but I think that I can manage to lift a corn chip or two." To demonstrate, she selected one of the broad corn chips from the basket, thrust it deep into the rich green, tomato-studded mound of guacamole and then popped the heavily laden chip into her mouth. "Mmmm!" She rolled her eyes in simulated ecstasy. "No one makes guacamole like Mom! Are you a guacamole fan?"

"It's one of my favorite things," Cane said as he gazed down at her lively face with an obvious appreciation of what he saw.

"Try some of this," Brianna invited huskily as she chose another chip. She loaded the second chip with another heaped scoop of guacamole and held it out to him. He bent his head to accept the offering, but his gaze never left her face. Her fingers brushed lightly past his lips while she fed him, in an almost compulsive gesture which was wholly foreign to her usual manner with men, let alone a man she had just met.

"It's good. It's very good," Cane spoke softly after he had chewed and swallowed.

His quiet voice seemed to release her from the thrall of an invisible anxiety, as though he had just bestowed a private reassurance, and she smiled up at him with a blinding, wordless radiance. Nothing like this had ever happened to her before, but she was *glad* she had come home! Perhaps Poopsie's imprudence on the raft was going to prove to have been the proverbial blessing in disguise, although eight pounds of smelly-wet poodle had been carrying Providence's disguise to ridiculous, not to mention painful, lengths!

Drew's usual boisterous entrance shattered the intimacy of the spell that Cane and Brianna had been weaving, oblivious to the astounded stares of her silently observing parents. "Hey, Bree, where'd you get the neat carving of the Appaloosa? It looks just like Beelzebub!"

Cane turned aside to set the tray he held on a low table in front of the couch, while Brianna gave her slightly bemused attention to her younger brother. "The carving? Oh, I found it in Oregon," she answered absentmindedly before she shook herself slightly, as though waking from the clinging enchantment of a dream. Her soft, unfocused stare sharpened and a familiar, teasing glint sparkled in the depths of her candid green eyes. "Actually"—she seemed to be considering the matter with a charmingly sober air of judicial seriousness—"now that I think about it, I don't know if the resemblance *is* all that strong. I had planned to give you the carving as a gift, but now that I've seen Beelzebub again, I realize that it doesn't do him justice. The ears aren't long enough and the carving just doesn't manage to convey properly his air of profound consideration—when he's considering just where he wants to take his next bite out of your hide. Still . . . if you can be satisfied with such an imperfect— Don't you throw that pillow at me, Andrew Kimball Graeme!" She yelped, knowing that she was far too sore to dodge any missiles her younger brother might heave at her provoking head.

Her ploy worked. Drew hesitated for the brief

moment Brianna needed. She strolled over to the couch, where her mother had taken a seat previously, and carefully lowered herself to sit beside her mother. With lofty poise, she then instructed regally, "Ignore the young barbarian, Cane. May I serve you a beer?"

Even the thwarted Drew had to laugh at Brianna's burlesque of a *grande dame* dispensing afternoon tea. By the governing family rules, laid down long ago by Mary and Adam to prevent sororicide and fratricide, he had been neatly outmaneuvered and must now admit that he'd lost that encounter hands down. He couldn't throw the pillow now and risk hitting his mother. He could only fume and plan a suitable revenge for the slighting reference to his beloved steed—Beelzebub did not have mule ears!—but his sister was unfortunately a well-practiced expert at avoiding his cunningly devised traps, both physical and verbal. It was practically impossible to disconcert her and she had a mischievous—and exasperating!—habit of turning a joke back on the joker.

He'd never even been able to exercise that natural and time-honored prerogative of all younger brothers: to tease and torment her about the continuous supply of boys who littered the place while she still lived at home. Because she hadn't cared for any of them as more than friends and casual dates, she'd been impervious to his taunts.

His father had often grumbled that the place was practically overrun by lovesick puppies who only came in handy at harvest time. Alex too had come in for his share of associative popularity, stemming from the time he had invited his sister to a college function as a date for a younger frater-

nity brother. From that time on, until he graduated, he never came home for vacation without
two or more of his friends in tow and he had once
confessed ruefully to Drew that, had he ever been
short of spending money at college, he could have
sold vacation slots to his eager friends and still
have had a waiting list! Brianna had remained
cheerfully, but kindly, immune to Alex's persuasive college contemporaries, as she had resisted
her own contemporaries' attempts to woo and win
her.

Brianna was sublimely unaware of the trend of
Drew's thought, although she had made a mental
note to watch out for his predictable attempts to
even the score. Granted, she and Alex did tend to
harp on Beelzebub's anatomical pecularities, when
really his ears were only the *teensiest* bit longer
than normal, but the horse hadn't been chris-
tened Beelzebub for nothing. He impartially nipped
at everyone, except for Drew, whom he tried to
follow around like an overgrown puppy when not
firmly tied or corralled. He also had an insatiable
appetite for her mother's carefully nurtured flowers and would devastate the vegetable garden whenever the opportunity presented itself, which tended
to be much oftener than any of them liked because the horse was fiendishly clever with locks
and stable door fastenings. If it hadn't been for
the fact that Drew had raised him from a colt,
bred out of his mother's favorite mare, Beelzebub
probably would have gone to meet his namesake,
packaged in a can. Drew had put in several sweaty,
back-breaking days of replanting the vegetable garden and flower borders on more than one occasion and . . .

"Oh Lord! Drew, where's Beelzebub? You rode him out to meet me, but you turned him loose during the excitement. Did you take him down to the stable after the rest of us came into the house?" Brianna's apprehensive questions got the immediate and appalled attention of her family.

"Andrew Kimball Graeme, if that animal has laid a lip on even one petal of my flowers, we'll serve him on the barbeque grill tonight, saddle and all, and you'll eat the saddle!" Mary promised grimly, her hazel eyes snapping.

Drew catapulted himself toward the door, only to carom off Alex's chest, which had just come through that same door.

"For crying out loud, Drew!" Alex barked, exasperated, as he reeled back against the door frame, trying to maintain his balance after the impact.

"Beelzebub!" Drew gasped, staggering grimly and determinedly forward. "I forgot all about him. *He's loose!*" This last was uttered in tones of deepest dread.

"Oh God," Alex groaned, and waved his brother through the door. "I'll head for the garden. You go down to the stable and hope that somebody down there saw him. Brianna, don't just sit there like a nit, laughing. If he's been in the garden again, Mom'll make dog meat of him for sure." He didn't wait to see if she was going to follow him, but took off after his brother with long strides. They heard the hard clatter of his boots echoing down the hall and the slam of the front door.

Brianna tried simultaneously to wipe her streaming eyes and hold her aching ribs, but found that she could accomplish neither very well. Since her ribs were more important, she clutched them and continued to whoop in a demented fashion. Mary wasn't smiling, but there was a suspicious compression of the muscles around Adam's mouth. Cane merely looked bewildered, although there had been a brief and hastily suppressed grin when Drew and Alex had collided in the Keystone Kaper at the door.

"Oooh. Aaah," Brianna moaned as she tried to catch her breath. "Poor Alex, he's going to be as black and blue as I am if Drew doesn't watch out," she gasped as she again mopped ineffectually at her damp cheeks with the back of one hand.

Cane picked up a napkin from the tray and crouched down beside her. With a broad palm under her chin, he tilted her face up and began to dry the tears of laughter which had rolled down her cheeks. "Do you always have such a devastating effect on your family?" he teased gently as he dabbed. "Perhaps you were up in Washington State several years ago when St. Helens blew?"

"Oh no," she denied gravely. "I take no responsibility whatsoever for natural disasters and Acts of God. And I hardly think it fair of you to blame me for Alex and Drew's latest collision because I was sitting right here the whole time, all the way across the room. Why, you were closer to the door than I was," she pointed out righteously.

"Yes, that's true," he admitted, in an obvious attempt to be strictly fair, "but I also distinctly remember Drew saying one time that 'things happen' when you're at home, and Brianna darlin', things have certainly been happening since you've been home."

His words and tones were softly teasing but his eyes were serious and Brianna was once again captured in the depths of his gaze. She and Cane were like two magnets, she thought hazily, and when they came within each other's critical field, the attraction became irresistible. *Something* certainly had happened to her since she had come home . . . and she could hardly wait to find out just what that something was!

Three

"Things might have been happening"—Adam responded to Cane's remark with a shake of his head—"but the one thing that *hasn't* happened is that I haven't yet gotten my beer. I'm very much afraid that I'm really going to need it before Alex comes back with that damage report." Suiting action to words, he wrapped a large hand around the handle of the nearest mug and lifted it to his lips.

Brianna hadn't missed Cane's look of bewilderment and so, between sips of her own beer, she explained about Beelzebub and his propensity for destruction. Cane's attractive slow smile was broadly evident by the time she had detailed *some* of the horse's lockpicking and flower eating escapades, from colthood on, as well as his single-minded devotion to Drew. " . . . And so we forgive him a lot, for Drew's sake, and besides," she concluded practically, "Drew always has to make good on the damage."

"Rather like the parent of a delinquent child," Cane observed, chuckling.

"Exactly," Brianna agreed, "except I'm afraid that this particular delinquent is never going to reform. The only solution seems to be to keep him locked up and just let him out in the custody of his parole officer."

"And speaking of the devil," Alex put in—he had entered the room during the last part of Brianna's comment to Cane—"both Drew and Mom's garden seem to have lucked out this time. Carlos saw Beelzebub hightailing it down toward the stable during all the commotion of Bree's arrival, so he grabbed him and stuck him in a stall. Drew's unsaddling him now and he'll be up directly." He assumed a plaintive expression. "Where's that cold beer I was promised? If anybody has earned one today, I sure have!"

By the time Drew was able to join the rest of his family, heavy inroads had been made into the chips, the guacamole and the salted peanuts . . . and the ice had melted in his orange soda. His mother took pity on her woebegone younger son and ordered kindly, "Go wash up, Drew. I'll get you a fresh soda and something to snack on. Then Brianna can tell us all what she's been doing."

Brianna knew exactly what her mother had in mind. With the ease of considerable practice, she started a mental review of her recent adventures, judiciously editing the more hair-raising episodes, shifting the emphasis to accentuate the humorous or merely exciting, glossing over the hazards and preparing to dwell on the spectacular scenery she'd seen. Her mother was a sucker for scenery.

Fortunately she'd already had some of her slides processed from the earlier rafting and kayaking segments of this particular project. They'd make a good distraction if the questions became uncomfortably specific. Even Poopsie could be turned to good account because that trip, ironically, had been the tamest of the lot. It had been just sheer bad chance that she'd gotten hurt.

Brianna had never lied to her family, and if ever they questioned her directly about the events of her trips, she answered the questions with complete candor. It was just better, for their peace of mind—and if she were to be completely honest, for hers as well—if they didn't ask. It upset them, especially her mother, to know about the risks she sometimes ran, but Brianna knew that they would never ask her to stop traveling and settle into an organized, prosaic and b-o-r-ing lifestyle. They loved her, they worried about her, but they wouldn't try to clip her wings, and for that she was profoundly grateful.

Brianna, her father and Alex chatted lightly while Mary and Drew were out of the room, with Cane as a silent but engrossed listener. His attention never wavered from Brianna's vivacious face, even while she was being brought up to date on the homely details of crop yields, number of calves dropped and other matters which are of paramount, even essential, interest to a farming family, but hardly the type of topic to encourage sparkling repartee.

Alex was enthusing about the young bull they had recently agreed to purchase when Mary came back into the room carrying Drew's refurbished orange soda in one hand and a large bowl of hot, buttered popcorn in the other. She handed both down to her youngest child, who had just dropped himself and his freshly scrubbed hands and face onto a large corduroy-covered beanbag chair moments before she had reentered the room.

"A little something to tide you over until dinner," she teased, fondly surveying the gangling length of his body as it overflowed the confines of the chair. Drew was going to be a big man, like his father and older brother, but at the moment he resembled nothing so much as a lanky but endearing puppy who had yet to fill out to match the potential of his frame and feet.

"Gee, thanks, Mom. A guy could starve to death around here as far as *some* people are concerned." The accusing and expressive glare Drew threw toward his brother, who was diligently scraping the last of the guacamole out of the bowl with a broken corn chip, was explicit and eloquent.

"When it comes to Mom's guacamole, it's every man for himself," Alex replied unfeelingly and popped the chip into his mouth.

Amid the light laughter provoked by Drew's expression of outrage as he watched his brother deliberately savor that last bite, Mary settled herself comfortably on the couch beside her daughter. An expectant pause followed. All eyes focused on Brianna.

Brianna grinned mischievously, folded her hands primly in her lap and intoned, "Perhaps you are wondering why I have called you all together here today . . ." and then deftly fielded and ate the plump piece of popcorn that Drew threw at her head. "Mmmm, that was better than a rotten tomato, I suppose, but I don't think that you are expressing a just appreciation of my dramatic talents, Drew. You didn't even give me a chance to announce that 'the butler done it' before you started registering your artistic criticism."

"This is going to turn into a murder all right, Bree, but there won't be any mystery about 'who-done-it' if you don't quit fooling around," Alex warned her with a threatening glint in his eyes. "How'd you come to crack yourself up this time?"

"Ah, now *that* was a case for justifiable homicide if ever there was one!" Brianna seized the opening gratefully. "You know that I've been working on a project about running the white water rivers, using kayaks, canoes and rafts. I even went on a tubing trip down the Sacramento River, just for contrast. Well, on the very last trip, the tamest of the lot, except for the tubing trip, I was done in by a pink poodle named Poopsie!"

She paused dramatically and swept a glance around her expectant audience. All were smiling slightly, prepared to be entertained. Except for Cane. He was lounging lazily in the comfortable armchair he had chosen specifically because it allowed him an unimpeded, full-face view of Brianna. He looked relaxed and at ease, but he wasn't smiling. His expression was interested, but serious and thoughtful and, so faintly that she couldn't be sure she was interpreting the nuance correctly, troubled.

Deliberately, instinctively coaxing, she met his gaze and smiled. She wanted to wipe away the trouble, whether it was imaginary or not. She wanted him to smile at her again with the secret message she had seen in his eyes, the message that was for their interpretation alone. She wanted . . .

Cane returned her smile, and there again was the message she had hoped to see, the warmth of a slow, stroking caress in the movement of his mouth. She felt as though he had somehow reached across the room and kissed her. A rich flood of delight spread throughout her body, but it didn't show dramatically on the barometer of the soft skin of her cheeks. It was only betrayed by the suddenly glowing green jewels of her eyes, which lit up as though someone had just focused a bright light so that it shown out through them.

"The poodle named Poopsie," Alex prompted, and Brianna realized that once again she'd forgotten about her onlooking family. They were probably wondering if she'd also suffered brain damage at the same time she had bruised her body!

With a distinct effort she pulled her gaze away from Cane and continued her interrupted narrative. "Ah, the unforgettable Poopsie." She grimaced. "Well, since I had spent most of my time on Class Three river runs, I thought I would finish up with a commercial trip on a Class Two run. There were five of us in the raft, not including Poopsie, who was on board solely courtesy of the well displayed depth of his Momsie's cleavage."

Well aware of the expressions of rank disbelief on her audience's faces, Brianna lifted her hand in a parody of solemn oath taking and said, "I kid you not. The lady identified herself as Poopsie's Momsie to us all. I would *never* make up something like that! I haven't yet figured out why in the world she wanted to take the rafting trip in the first place, because she certainly wasn't the outdoor type, but she was most insistent that both she and Poopsie go. The guide, who was unfortunately also the proprietor of the raft, had a speculative eye on the open top buttons of Momsie's shirt and couldn't be said to have been exercising his best professional judgment." Here Brianna rolled her eyes expressively. Alex choked slightly and her father sternly suppressed a smile. She didn't look over at Cane.

"Anyway, when Momsie insisted that she wouldn't go unless her darling Poopsie was allowed to go too, and when she also pointed out that there was no one to leave the little darling with, the guide regrettably allowed his baser instincts, and probably his hopes for the evening—which I am positive involved Momsie sans Poopsie, her cleavage, and maybe a bottle of wine—to outweigh his common sense. Poopsie came with us.

"Unfortunately Poopsie also panicked when Momsie got an unexpected—to her—faceful of water from a wave. She screamed like a steam calliope. He abandoned ship right in the middle of the river and, in spite of the fact that poodles as a breed are supposed to be both intelligent and at home in the water, Poopsie disgraced his genetic heritage and promptly began to drown. *I* then made the mistake of allowing my instincts to outweigh my good sense and went in after him. He bit me—the ungrateful whelp!—and I collided with several rocks in the course of the rescue, but eventually we both got back to the raft and completed the trip, somewhat the worse for wear all around. His coiffure and pink dye job will never be the same."

Brianna made an exaggerated face of mocking dismay. "It was a singularly ignominious conclusion to what had been a delightful and exciting project. And the worst of it is that I probably won't be able to use Momsie as material for a humorous article because she's just the type who'd sue me, and she's such a vivid—did I mention that she had pink hair too?—type that there's no disguising her!" Bree's expression of chagrin elicited sympathetic laughter.

Well satisfied with the way she had managed to brush past the necessary explanation of how she had come to dent herself, Brianna went on to wax eloquent about some of the less hair-raising aspects of her other river rides, promising a showing of the slides she had with her, including suitable commentary. She answered Drew's questions about her reference to the river classification, explaining that it referred to ranking rivers according to their condition and degree of difficulty, including types and severity of rapids, and whether they had to be scouted from shore before the attempt to run them could be made. She didn't mention that it also referred to the degree of difficulty of rescue conditions. That was not something to dwell on, and besides, she had come home safely, hadn't she? That was all that really mattered.

After the hungry horde had wolfed down all the snacks that Mary had prepared, Brianna excused herself with the ostensible intention of showering her dusty, travel-weary body. She did indeed intend to shower and change into fresh clothes, but even more urgently she thought she needed a quiet moment to sort out her turbulent and, if the truth be admitted, rather dazed emotional state. Nothing like Cane Taylor had ever happened to her before.

In spite of the fact that there had always been a plentiful—one might even go so far as to say an overabundant—supply of masculine attention in Brianna's life, she had resolutely remained romantically elusive and heart-whole. Even though a number of men had already tried their best to convince her that she was the flame that attracts the enthralled moth—and each had expressed an eager willingness to volunteer for the role of moth! —Brianna had never felt the slightest desire to even *singe* anyone. Until now.

And now? From the very first moment her eyes had met Cane's smiling blue gaze, little hot flames of excitement and anticipation had begun to dance a frenzied, fervent jig atop every corpuscle, both red *and* white, in her body! She could feel her temperature rising, but it wasn't a change in Fahrenheit degrees that could be measured by a thread of mercury rising in a thin glass tube. She had the classic symptoms all right, Brianna thought cheerfully as she peered at her reflection in the bathroom mirror just before she took her shower: overbright eyes, a flushed face and—she laid a slender, monitoring finger against the side of her tanned throat—a racing pulse. How intriguing that both the cause and cure for this particular fever were embodied in the lanky length of the blue-eyed stranger who, to her discerning heart, was no stranger at all. She had known him from the moment she'd seen him and—she smiled with serene certainty as she stepped beneath the steamy warmth of the shower spray—she was no stranger to him either. His eyes had been eloquent with recognition.

And Cane's eyes were eloquent with masculine appreciation when she came back out to join the rest of the family on the patio at the rear of the house, where they were barbecuing steaks, not Beelzebub. She had dressed in white, tight, fringed cut-offs and a vividly flowered cotton shirt, tucked down inside the shorts to cover the bruises which splotched the smooth skin over her ribs. Normally she wore this particular shirt knotted high beneath her full breasts, but that would be inadvisable for some time to come. The pale green background of the shirt intensified the flirting green of her eyes as they sparkled at Cane from behind the dark fan of her black, curling eyelashes, and the lush coral of several of the splashy flowers scattered at random over the shirt was repeated in the glow of the gloss frosting her delectably curved mouth.

While Adam, Alex and Drew hovered hungrily and watchfully around the smoking brick grill, like anxious sorcerers overseeing the delicate transmutation of base metal into precious gold, Cane moved toward Brianna as she opened the sliding glass door which separated the family room from the patio and stepped through. His keen, appreciative gaze moved thoroughly and slowly over every inch of her but his searching inspection didn't embarrass or discomfit her—she *liked* having Cane look at her—until, that is, his eyes unerringly found the one small bruise, high on the outside of her thigh, that was half hidden by the soft thread fringe of her cut-offs. She had thought it would be unnoticeable, and so it would have been, to any casual scrutiny. But Cane hadn't examined every visible inch of her skin with cursory attention!

Slowly, as though he didn't want to make any sudden moves which might startle her into a precipitate flight, Cane's hand lifted from his side and with one gentle finger, brushed aside the fringe and lightly stroked over the dark mark with its little hard knot of tissue beneath the skin. "The tip of the iceberg?" he asked tightly. The strangely ragged edge to the brief question gave his deep, pleasant voice a harsh timbre.

Brianna swallowed thickly through a suddenly tight throat before she tried to frame a light answer. She could swear that there was an actual shadow of pain darkening those clear blue eyes! "Would you believe a beauty mark?" she queried fliply.

"No." His voice wasn't ragged anymore. It was just grim.

"Oh." She looked up at him through her lashes. "I heal very quickly," she offered placatingly.

He wasn't noticeably appeased. "That's fortunate," Cane responded dryly, "but one might be allowed to wish that you didn't have to utilize that ability quite so often."

Brianna's mouth fell open. He was . . . he was *scolding* her! She stared up at him with a look of absolute stupefaction, which quickly began to change to one of sharp irritation. *No one* had the right to scold her and she was just about to tell Mr. Cane Taylor so in words of ten syllables or more, perhaps interspersed with a few pithy one- and two-syllable expressions to add the proper impact.

Before she could close her mouth and open it again to begin, Cane's mouth curved up into a smile of great sweetness but no noticeable penitence. "Don't peck me, little wild bird," he said, laughter moving in his voice. "Let me smooth down those ruffled feathers."

He ran his wide-spread fingers through the short soft black curls which waved in glossy abandon over her beautifully shaped skull. The thick curling tendrils twined around his long fingers as though reluctant to release him from their soft snare. He drew his hand out slowly as though equally loath to be freed from his voluntary captivity.

"Your mother made some more guacamole," he said switching subjects smoothly. His hand slid down the side of her neck, trailed across her shoulder and slipped down her arm to capture her hand and twine the fingers with his own warm ones. He tugged gently. "Come, Brianna. Let me tempt you."

"You already have," Brianna thought shakenly as she obediently walked beside him to the table where her mother had decoratively arranged a selection of side dishes to complement and accompany the succulent, tender steaks.

Not releasing her captive hand, Cane used his free hand to heap a corn chip with a moist mound of the guacamole and then lift it and hold it poised before her mouth. "Open, wary little wild bird," he ordered softly. "Learn to eat from my hand."

"Aren't you afraid that I might be prone to bite the hand that feeds me?" Brianna responded tartly.

"Then you'd have to kiss it and make it well," was his swift topper to her cliché. "I'll take that chance any day. Bite away," he challenged deliberately.

It was not a game Brianna had bothered to play

before, but her instincts were all in excellent working order. With the softest and most careful of touches she lipped the laden chip into her mouth and then, with a quick sideways movement of her head, she pinched the pad of his forefinger in a sharp, swift nip with her teeth. After she had calmly chewed and swallowed the chip he had fed her, she sweetly informed Cane, "It's sometimes dangerous to dare a Graeme. We're not noted for stepping back from a challenge. Now shall I kiss it and make it well?"

Cane ostentatiously counted each finger on the abused hand before he held it out to Brianna, forefinger gingerly extended, for her healing ministrations. "I suppose I can spare one," he allowed doubtfully, his eyes vividly blue with mockery. Then his expression shifted to anxious gravity. "Will you be able to save the finger, doctor? And will I have to have a rabies shot? I'm not at all sure whether the vixen who bit me has had all of her proper inoculations. In fact, for safety's sake, I think that it will be necessary for me to keep her under close observation to see what develops. I can already feel myself succumbing to an incurable ailment."

Brianna gently kissed the finger she had bitten, her lips moving comfortingly against the unmarked flesh. "It sounds serious, Mr. Taylor," she said gravely. "Do you think your affliction is liable to prove infectious?"

He brushed the miraculously healed finger across her lips softly before he dropped his hand to his side and reassured her, "Oh, I'm sure that we will be able to restrict the contagion, Miss Graeme. This particular disease has its limits: it claims only two victims at a time." He heaved an exaggerated sigh. "For those two victims, however, I can hold out little hope. This remarkable virus has no known cure and all that can be done for the sufferers is to make them comfortable. The prescription calls for frequent and regular doses of TLC, mutually administered." He smiled down at her with coaxing charm. "And this particular strain seems to be especially swift-striking and virulent, wouldn't you say? I think we should begin treatment as promptly as possible."

No one had ever listed indecisiveness or overcautiousness as particular faults of Brianna's. She smiled happily up at Cane and agreed, "A *very* virulent strain, it would seem. I, however, have had no previous experience with the disease," she admitted candidly. "I must bow to your greater experience on the subject." There was the faintest questioning challenge in her voice.

Cane was equal to the challenge. All traces of humor and teasing were wiped from his expression and voice. His next words were softly serious. "I've recognized the symptoms of the malady through instinct, not experience, Brianna," he responded evenly. Then his slow, attractive smile spread across his face again. He concluded lightly, "One other important characteristic of this disease that I didn't mention before is that it strikes each victim just once in a lifetime. Some unlucky people never catch it, even in its mildest form, but once you *have* contracted it, you've caught it for life. There isn't any remedy."

Cane didn't seem to be in the least perturbed by the possibility of their having contracted an incurable illness, Brianna reflected contentedly. If anything, his attitude might best be described as one of dazed, even slightly disbelieving, elation. But then, she acknowledged silently, with the clear-eyed candor which was such an integral element of her personality, she too seemed to be caught inescapably in the grip of some reckless euphoria.

The heady emotion coursing through her body might seem to be a close kin to those elated feelings that she always experienced whenever she indulged her bent for hazardous pursuits, but this particular sensation was, she strongly suspected, unique . . . and quite possibly dangerously addictive! She felt as though she had suddenly—and certainly unexpectedly!—been thrust into a headlong race down a particularly turbulent stretch of wildwater. She was exhilarated, enraptured and exuberantly intoxicated, and she was racing rashly toward . . . what? This was uncharted territory for her.

Cane had called her "wild bird" and perhaps his teasing words were far more appropriate than he could have imagined or intended. She had always flown free, unrestricted by hood or leash, returning to the family nest at her own will and in her own time, never subject to the bidding and binding of another. Like a falcon spiraling steadily up into the high freedom of the sky, there to wheel and soar in a celebration of glorious independence, she had flown far and, by choice, had always flown alone. Not for her had there been the silken tangle of the falconer's net, no matter how attractively baited the proffered lures had been. No bait had been worth the price—the loss of her treasured freedom.

But the attraction of Cane's lure was one she had neither the desire nor the intention of resisting! When he asked quietly "Will you have dinner with me tomorrow night?" she didn't hesitate. "I'd love to," she said happily . . . and immediately. The way she felt right now, if he hadn't asked her, she would have asked him!

"Hey, Bree! Tell Mom that the steaks are ready," Alex's call reminded Brianna and Cane that they weren't alone. "If, that is, you haven't lost interest in something as ordinary as food," he jibed pointedly.

"Subtle, brother Alex, really subtle," Brianna muttered as she left Cane. She knew that she was going to have to take a lot of teasing from the men in her family, but she hadn't expected it to start so soon.

Four

The teasing started sooner than Brianna expected, but it ended much sooner than either of her brothers had planned. It ended, in fact, when they discovered that her instinctive defensive strategy was disconcertingly effective against their most determined assaults. Drew, ever the impetuous youth, was the first to blunt his thrust against her armor. His attempt to even the score on Beelzebub's behalf came when he accosted her at the edge of the patio, away from Cane and the rest of the family, and provocatively chanted in a whisper only she could hear, "Bree's got a boyfriend. Bree's got a boyfriend."

His gleeful parody of grammar school taunts elicited a deflating response from his imperturbable sister. She smiled happily and admitted smugly, "Yes, I do believe you're right, and don't you think it's about time? After all, you don't want to have to keep introducing me to all your friends as your old maid sister, do you?" She patted his cheek lightly and laughed huskily at his disgruntled expression before strolling away to join Cane where he stood chatting with her mother and father.

Alex was the next unsuspecting unfortunate. He chose his moment at the breakfast table the next morning, just after Brianna informed her mother not to expect her for supper that night because she had a date with Cane. Alex wasn't allowed more than a preliminary "We might well begin to wonder if you came home to see us or Cane . . ." before she cut him off neatly at the knees with a crisp "Brother dear, if I had known Cane existed, you can bet I would have come home a month ago!"

Mary swallowed her smile and her mouthful of pancakes. Not for nothing had she taught her daughter that the best defense against a brother's teasing is a good offense! Alex's jaw dropped in a most satisfactory fashion and he developed a sudden and intense interest in the sports section of the morning newspaper. Brianna grinned cherubically and winked at her mother, woman-to-woman, before continuing calmly, "Mom, I have some errands in town this morning. What needs picking up?" It was common practice for anyone having business in town to run any necessary errands for the ranch at the same time, unless particularly pressed for time, and Brianna automatically adjusted her schedule to accommodate the long familiar routine.

She casually tucked behind the sun visor the short list furnished by her mother and the mail for the post office, flicked on the cassette tape deck to release the rich, whiskey-rough tones of a

Kenny Rogers tape lamenting a faithless wife, and carefully guided the Blazer over the oft-traveled unpaved ranch road and then, at a greatly increased speed, onto the smoothly paved road leading into town. Her private errand shouldn't take up much time, she mused silently as she swung the heavy vehicle into a graceful sweep around a sharp curve, if, that is, Dr. Joe's nurse could work her into his morning schedule. Her mother's "do" list shouldn't pose any problem either since it seemed to be composed mainly of items such as "pick up Adam's brown suit from cleaners" and "get six skeins light blue rug yarn at Knit 'n Needle shop." She would be home for lunch with time to spare.

Her well-intentioned plans, alas, didn't take into account the time-consuming effect of a number of unexpected encounters with friends, who were delighted to discover that she had come home for a while. She shared a quick cola with one friend—female—and tactfully turned down dates with two others—male—and finally escaped only by promising everyone else who wanted to detain her that they'd all get together soon at a cookout at the ranch. The Graemes were justly renowned for their hospitality and invitations to their barbecues were eagerly accepted. Adam's recipe for hot hickory sauce was widely admired and jealously coveted but it remained a Graeme family secret. Brianna was confident that her mother really wouldn't mind, even though her impulsive daughter had just committed the family to the effort involved in giving a major party. Mary loved to entertain.

And it would be the perfect opportunity for her friends to meet Cane, Brianna reflected with satisfaction. Not that she planned to show him off, exactly—Cane wasn't some sort of prize to be displayed!—but he was new to the area and his main contacts to date had been work-oriented. He must have been lonely.

Her mouth curved into an anticipatory smile as she sped homeward. Of course, she was going to make sure that Cane wasn't lonely any more, but still, it would be nice for him to have an entrée into the social life of the community. The cultural life of the immediate area was somewhat limited in scope. Most of the local residents depended on trips into San Francisco and its environs for plays, concerts and the celebration of special occasions, but, if you knew where to find it, there was a lot of impromptu and low-key entertainment, of the sort Brianna instinctively knew Cane would enjoy, available locally on an ongoing basis. Sally, the friend with whom she'd shared the cola, had mentioned a surprise birthday party, a water skiing outing and a group going roller skating, all to take place within a week's time, all activities which Brianna knew she'd be urged to attend as soon as the various hosts discovered that she was home.

She wondered if Cane knew how to roller skate? There was so much to discover about him, she anticipated pleasurably, and *not* just the extent of his prowess on eight wheels! He had the confident look of a man who was adept at a lot of things and she could hardly wait to begin exploring the full range of his capabilities. She was good at a lot of things too and, as for the things she hadn't learned yet, she knew she'd surely enjoy letting Cane teach her!

Mary was the type of mother every girl should

have. She had instructed Alex to invite Cane up to the house to share the midday meal with the family. Cane, who was not about to pass up an opportunity to see Brianna *and* to enjoy a meal he hadn't had to prepare himself, had accepted Alex's invitation readily. Brianna discovered this happy surprise when she walked into the dining room, carrying the mail she had collected in town. She was late and they had started without her, but since they had only just begun, there were still a few scattered scraps and crusts left with which to assuage her hunger.

"Sorry I'm late, Mom," she apologized. "Keep your fork out of that last chicken leg, Andrew Graeme. It's mine. You've already got two on your plate. Take a couple of those wings or an extra helping of the carrots and peas if you're all that ravenous," she added briskly, without pausing for breath, automatically claiming and defending her share of the noontime meal from Drew's greedy assault.

"Dad, here's the mail from town. I'll wash my hands and *be right back.*" The last three words were heavily emphasized and directed toward Andrew.

"I'll defend your claim, Brianna," Cane volunteered helpfully. "Your leg will be safe with me." He maintained a perfectly sober expression but his eyes danced with lazy deviltry, inviting her private interpretation of his silent, personal message.

A number of responses, ranging from the slightly risqué to the outright ribald, trembled on her tongue, but she sternly suppressed them all. Her mother's dining room wasn't the place, nor, with

Drew's adolescent ears aflap, was this the time. She contented herself with a *speaking* look and a sedate "Thank you, Cane. I appreciate your offer and I commend your courage. I'll only be a moment. Hold the fort."

She laid the mail beside her father's plate and whisked into the kitchen to wash her hands. *"Bless you, Mother dear,"* she murmured inaudibly while the water ran down her wrists, rinsing away the soap. *"I think I owe you half a dozen more roses on your next birthday."*

She hadn't forgotten a thing about Cane overnight. His eyes were still the same rich blue, his hair the remembered shade of sun-tipped golden brown and the mere sight of his lean face made her heart want to do a dozen anatomically impossible things. Oh, he tempted her all right! She wanted to walk over to him, curl up in his lap and smooth the soft blue denim of his work shirt across the width of his shoulders and down the broad planes of his chest. She wanted to feel the whipcord strength of his arms as they encircled her, capturing her and pulling her inescapably against the deep, muscled arch of his rib cage, holding her willingly in thrall while his lips whispered and wandered, tracing and tasting the texture of her skin.

A shivering warmth rippled over her body and she laughed softly to herself as she towel dried her dripping hands. If she didn't put a quick curb on her rampaging imagination, the next thing she knew, she'd be rushing into her mother's dining room to attack Cane at the table where he sat peacefully and unsuspectingly eating his meal.

And while *he* probably wouldn't object, her father certainly would!

And Alex would never let her live it down. Brianna, the Blissfully Unbridled. Alex had more than once likened her to a mustang filly, skittishly suspicious of the slightest attempt to curb her precious freedom. Lo, how the mighty are fallen! Here she was, practically begging for a halter and the hobbles, just as long as Cane was the one who put them on her.

She arranged her expression into something resembling propriety and rejoined her family and Cane. Cane rose immediately to pull out her chair and, obviously not a man to let an opportunity pass, additionally contrived to stroke the tips of his fingers across the back of her shoulders under the guise of positioning her chair at the table. It was a light yet firm touch that said: "I'm here." Brianna decided that he evidently believed in the value of nonverbal communication through body language and, moreover, spoke the language so well that she wasn't going to need to ask for a translation. Delightful!

Cane had successfully defended her chicken leg, and a thigh as well. The conversation around the table paused politely while she filled her plate with meat and vegetables and accepted the tall glass of sun-brewed iced tea that her father poured and passed down to her. She took a few preliminary bites, just to catch up with the rest of the family, and then answered Alex's shrewd "Run into a lot of people in town?" with a wry "Did I ever! Why do you think I'm late for lunch?"

"Did you happen to run into either Steve Delaray or Cord Roberts?" Alex asked with bland innocence. "I just happened to mention that you were coming home when I saw them a couple of days ago at the hardware store in town. They both . . . ah . . . seemed pretty pleased to hear it."

"Cute, brother, really cute," Brianna thought with some asperity. *"You just don't know when to give it a rest, do you? But you're going to get yours some day and, brother, am I going to enjoy every minute of it! If I'm lucky, I'll even be right there in a ringside seat when it finally happens to you."*

She flicked a glance at her brother that should have made his intractably straight hair curl like springs and then looked over at Cane. He was watching the byplay, and her, with considerable interest, a crinkle of amusement creasing the corners of his eyes. She allowed her gaze to lock with his as she answered Alex's question. "I saw Cord," she admitted indifferently, dismissively, closing the subject with a tone which dripped boredom.

"And?" Alex prodded.

"'Yours' will have buck teeth and knock-knees, Alex Graeme," she vowed silently through gritted teeth. *"I will personally see to it!"*

"I told him I was busy," she announced clearly and smiled at Cane with deliberate intimacy. "Very busy."

Cane smiled his slow, wide smile and affirmed with soft satisfaction, "Very busy." A deep sensual fire flared briefly but unmistakably, like the hottest of blue flames, in his look, which roved caressingly over the planes of her face.

"I did, however, invite him and a number of other people to a barbeque, date to be decided later," Brianna announced conversationally to the table in general. "That's okay with you, isn't it, Mom?" she queried, happily confident that her mother wouldn't fail her.

And of course Mary didn't.

"Certainly, dear. That's an excellent idea. We haven't given a party for quite a while and it'll enable me to repay a number of obligations all at one time. A barbeque will serve the purpose admirably," Mary said enthusiastically.

Adam sighed with resignation. "Just tell me how much beef you'll need and when you want the pit dug." He accepted his usual responsibility for the parties his wife planned. "Will you want me to order a pig from Johnny Sevier as well?" When Mary planned a barbeque, she planned a *barbeque*!

"Mmmm." His wife pursed her lips thoughtfully. "Probably. Bree and I will start making out the guest list this afternoon. I'll let you know by dinnertime." She began to eat steadily, but with an abstracted air.

Alex groaned theatrically. "We're in for it now," he advised Cane sadly. "Mom's grandfather was a general in the army. She took lessons at his knee on how to mobilize the troops and I feel honor-bound to warn you that Mom considers any warm body within range a legitimate conscript whenever she's planning a party. You too can find yourself sweating buckets while digging a barbeque pit in the hot sun if you play your cards wrong. Not that we won't welcome the additional muscle power," he concluded expressively.

"No sweat," Cane punned. "I happen to know where we can borrow a backhoe." He exchanged a glance of masculine conspiracy with Adam, Alex and Drew.

"You're a man after my own heart," Alex announced in satisfied tones.

Brianna grinned down at her plate. Her sentiments exactly!

Either Cane could read her mind or perhaps he merely felt her shoulders shaking as she laughed silently because he leaned closer to her and murmured quietly, "Dare I hope that Alex's statement might represent a family consensus?"

"Since I don't have a sister who'd be competition, you may," she whispered demurely. "Feel free to charm my whole family."

"You don't have any competition. You could have a hundred sisters and it wouldn't make the slightest difference."

It was a lovely compliment and the properly gracious response trembled momentarily on Brianna's full lips, but then her reprehensible sense of humor got the better of her. A chuckle gurgled in her throat as she fought the brief battle and lost. "It would have made a heck of a difference to my mother," she pointed out pertly.

Cane grimaced with comical disgust. "Ouch. So much for trying to pay a graceful compliment." He cocked a stern eye at her. "Maybe I should just forget the compliments and depend on direct tactics. I do believe that I've still got my old club and a saber-toothed tiger skin ensemble somewhere in my closet. Shall I dig them out and dust them off? Are you an old-fashioned girl?"

Brianna rubbed her fingers soothingly across her scalp and was glad she wore her hair short. "I'm not *that* old-fashioned," she muttered. "And of course you have to remember that there aren't many caves in this part of the country. Besides, whatever mastodons you could find nowadays would make pretty bony eating." Her eyes swept over his torso appraisingly, bright mischief sparkling in her green gaze. "Although I'll bet you'd look quite impressive draped in a tiger skin, with your trusty club resting across your shoulder. Perhaps . . ." She allowed her voice to trail away thoughtfully before concluding with a deeply regretful sigh, "No, I suppose not. I guess you'd better just stick to the compliments."

A deep growl rumbled softly in Cane's chest and Brianna reached over to pat his sinewy arm lightly. "Now, now," she soothed. "It won't be so bad. You'll see. I'm willing to devote a considerable amount of time to the project and I'm sure you have a strong natural talent." She assumed a gallant expression denoting heroic self-sacrifice. "We'll practice and practice until you've . . . er . . . mastered the technique."

"Now that's mighty generous of you, Brianna honey," Cane drawled dangerously. "I can hardly wait to start my lessons in the technique of . . . mastery." His drawl deepened. "I can also assure you that I'm more than willing to practice and practice on . . . er . . . with you until I get it right." His grin was a manifestation of sheer masculine anticipation.

Brianna acknowledged Cane's "mastery" in this particular verbal encounter with a rueful chuckle. "One up to you, Cane. I concede that the use of a club would be wholly superfluous. You wield a mean riposte. I cry quarter."

Brianna's family was rapidly becoming accustomed, one might even say resigned, to being ignored whenever she focused on Cane. They had listened but they had also continued to eat, and now Adam slid his chair back from the table and excused himself to his wife with a "Delicious lunch as always, Mary darling. I've got an appointment with Al Lomax in half an hour so I'd better get going." He dropped a brief, customary kiss on her hair, nodded generally to everyone else and left the room, carrying his plate. Mary had trained her men well.

Alex and Drew also began to make motions of departure stacking their own plates and flatware and gathering the serving bowls. Drew, emboldened by the fact that his older brother hadn't fared too badly at their sister's hands, couldn't resist the temptation of a parting thrust. He surveyed Brianna's as yet barely touched plate and admonished her reproachfully, "Gee, Bree, if you weren't really going to eat that chicken leg, you could have let me have it. I'm a growing boy and you've probably just knocked a whole inch off my potential height owing to malnutrition. My basketball coach won't be pleased, let me tell you. He was going to start me at center next year and now I bet I'll be warming the bench the whole season, all because your eyes were bigger than your stomach."

Brianna picked up the disputed chicken leg and deliberately took a large bite out of it, staring narrow-eyed at her provocative younger brother. Starch for his jockey shorts at the very least, she decided with cool calculation.

" 'Your eyes were bigger than your stomach?' "

Cane repeated questioningly. "I don't believe I've ever heard that particular expression before."

Brianna chewed and swallowed. "That's one of Mom's sayings," she explained obligingly. "We usually heard it whenever Mom and Dad took us to dinner at a cafeteria or a restaurant that served meals buffet-style, if Mom thought we were getting carried away by the extravagance of choice, filling our plates with more food than we could comfortably consume. The family rule has always been: 'What you take, you eat.' But somehow, when we ate at a cafeteria, our greed regularly seemed to outstrip our abilities and Mom would murmur meaningfully 'Are your eyes bigger than your stomachs?' as we took helpings of everything in sight. Even today I have trouble accurately estimating my capacity whenever I'm confronted by all those lovely selections of a buffet. I suppose it probably stems from an obscure, primitive instinct to gorge in times of plenty. I guess that if I were a horse, I'd probably have foundered a long time ago."

"Well, that takes care of my choice of a restaurant for tonight," Cane decided whimsically. "I know the perfect one to appeal to the glutton in you and once I've fed you past satisfaction, you won't be able to run very fast when I chase you."

"My very dear man," Brianna purred throatily, feigning wide-eyed disbelief, "how ever did you come by the incredible notion that I might want to run away from you in the first place?"

She had won that verbal joust on points, Brianna reflected with some satisfaction as she briskly dried her water-spangled body with a thick towel. Of course Cane knew full well—as did her whole family by now!—that he wouldn't have to pursue her. You can't chase someone who isn't running.

She stretched experimentally and smiled like some species of sensual Cheshire cat as she massaged scented body lotion into her skin with long slow strokes. It *was* a good thing she healed rapidly. The bruises were fading nicely, although not yet completely gone, and a good deal of the stiffness from her pulled muscles had loosened with judicious, gentle exercise. A few more days should see her completely over the effects of the accident. Lucky accident. Actually she hadn't planned to come home for several more months, and what a waste of time that would have been!

Her parents plainly approved of Cane, she thought contentedly as she slipped into the lacy scraps of nothing which masqueraded under the common name of underwear. They hadn't actually said it in so many words, but had they not liked him, her mother would never have invited him to share the family's midday meal, a tacit indication of acceptance. But of course they liked him. How could they not? He was Cane. He was her choice.

Deftly her fingers manipulated the zipper of her dress and then smoothed the tender leaf green of the soft cotton fabric down over the line of her hips. Her friends would like him too, or at least, she amended with a silent chuckle, the feminine portion of her world of acquaintances would. The masculine contingent would come around too, eventually, because Cane was the type of man whom other men, thwarted suitors included, both liked and respected. And they'd all get the chance, male and female, because between them, she and her mother had invited just about everyone they knew in both valleys on either side of the Altamont Pass. It would definitely take a pig from Johnny Sevier, and she hoped Cane hadn't been kidding when he said he knew where to get hold of a backhoe, because it would probably take two pits as well. She could hear Alex's moans and groans already.

To tell the truth, though, Brianna thought with some bewilderment as she brushed on eyeshadow and smoothed on lip gloss, she hadn't really expected the party to mushroom into such alarming proportions. Her mother seemed to have gotten the bit firmly between her teeth and this afternoon, as they had compiled the guest list, she had told Brianna to invite EVERYBODY.

Brianna flexed her fingers ruefully. It had been like typing up the Oakland phone book by the time she had finished the lists of names, addresses and phone numbers. Fortunately her mother's bridge club would help with the invitations and at the party itself. They were all experienced party givers and had long ago formed a mutual aid society which swung into action whenever one of the members decided to throw a major bash. There'd still be plenty for her to do—after all, she had gotten them all into this, Brianna admitted fairly—but it wasn't as bad as it could have been, she reassured herself hopefully. She lacked her mother's excessive enthusiasm for party planning and giving.

Anyway, she'd worry about the party tomorrow. Tonight she had other, more important things to think about. Like which perfume would be her best choice if she wanted to drive Cane absolutely wild? She selected, sprayed and dabbed and then sniffed with satisfaction. Scientists were now studying the uses of pheromones to attract and repel in both the insect and animal kingdoms, but the smart woman had always known the value of a come-hither scent.

When Cane's knock cracked crisply against the solid wood of the front door, she felt a surge of excitement and anticipation which was akin to, but even more intense than, the one which had swept through her while she was successfully maneuvering her kayak through a tricky stretch of rapids during her first solo trip down a wild river. She started toward the door, a spring of eagerness evident in each step. He was right on time but she felt as though she had been waiting for him forever.

From behind her, Drew's voice rang out clearly. "Would you like me to answer the door for you, Bree?"

She paused and glanced back over her shoulder at him. He had risen from the chair where he had been comfortably sprawled reading a science-fiction paperback book and was now trying to look both innocent and helpful. He managed neither successfully.

"Go play in the street, little brother," she advised kindly and kept on walking toward the front door. Drew laughed softly behind her, delighted to have gotten a rise out of her at last.

With unabashed eagerness, Brianna twisted the doorknob and swung the door wide. Her greeting to Cane was a prosaic "Hello, Cane." But the welcome of her smile mocked the sedateness of her words, as did the quick hand she stretched out to clasp and entwine with his lean, sunbrowned fingers. They didn't need the words. The pressure of their handclasp said it all.

"I'm all ready," she announced proudly. Punctuality was one of her lesser lauded virtues, according to the men of her family. "Come on in and we'll say 'bye to the folks. Mom's in the kitchen fixing supper and Dad's watching the national news on the TV in the family room."

Suiting actions to words, she started to lead him down the hall, pulling on his hand like a dainty tug striving to overcome the inertia of a larger vessel. Cane resisted the pull briefly while he paused to shut the front door, but then he obediently yielded to her insistent guidance. Brianna was determined to keep the hellos and goodbyes to the polite minimums, and she twitched Cane's hand in warning when it seemed as though he might be going to courteously accept her father's offer of a cold beer.

She did love her family dearly and relished their lively companionship at any time, as long as the time was tomorrow. Her father had just as strong a sense of mischief as did his sons and he had been suspiciously and uncharacteristically discreet in his reaction to his daughter's unprecedented preoccupation with Cane. Brianna didn't deceive herself that his discretion was in any way due to some delicate fatherly consideration for her presumably tender sensibilities. He was just waiting for the best opportunity.

Alex and Drew were mere callow, impetuous youths. Her father knew how to bide his time and choose the proper moment. It would be just like him to maneuver an unsuspecting Cane into having their meal with the family tonight and then cunningly whittle away at the rest of the evening with the challenge of a game—or three—of pool (which Brianna already knew Cane played and enjoyed) until Cane once again was saying goodnight to her on the front porch under the benign—and damnably inconvenient—chaperonage of her whole family!

Not if her name was Brianna Elizabeth Graeme, she vowed determinedly. The propensity for teasing might be specifically located in the DNA of the masculine genes of her family lineage, but for virtuoso, one-step-ahead-of-you connivance, she'd rely every time on the feminine genes handed down from mother to daughter, generation after generation, on the distaff line. It was better to be safe—and perhaps unwontedly suspicious—than to be unkissed!

As she hurried Cane back down the hall and out the front door he quipped, "Hey, what's the rush? Did the house catch on fire? Don't you think we ought to try to rescue your family too?"

"Not unless you want to kiss me goodnight in front of an appreciative audience tonight," Brianna returned bluntly.

"What?"

"My father is a devious man," Brianna explained succinctly. "Don't be misled by that kindly, weatherbeaten face. He's a far worse tease than either of my brothers—in fact, he taught them how—and he's far more subtle. He would consider it a marvelous joke to inveigle us into staying at home tonight *en famille* and afterwards we'd all wave goodbye to you from the front porch when the evening was over. Get the picture?"

"Vividly." Cane's stride lengthened and Brianna had to half-skip to keep up. "My older brother has a sense of humor like that. There is no cure," he added sadly. "It's an affliction, a quirk in the brain, that they're born with and all you can do is stay fast on your feet around them."

"Well, let's not carry it to ridiculous extremes," Brianna panted laughingly as she tried to match Cane's long strides. "I don't think we need to be *this* fast."

"Ah, but I don't plan to let anything interfere with my goodnight kiss," Cane announced as he ruthlessly hustled her toward his truck. "I'm taking no chances."

He opened the door of the truck and boosted her up onto the bench seat with a smooth, easy motion, as though she routinely breathed helium instead of oxygen. He gently pushed the skirt of her dress out of the way, cautioned "Watch out for the door," pressed the locking button down and closed the truck's door with a small slam.

"Whoosh." Brianna breathed in a laughing sigh. When Cane took charge, he definitely took charge.

Cane strode briskly around to the driver's side, opened the door and climbed in. He settled behind the wheel and proclaimed with villainous satisfaction, "And now I'm going to whisk you away to a high tower in my castle. You're totally in my power, fair maid. Buckle up."

The sober instruction after the flight of fancy set Brianna laughing again. "You're not taking this abduction in the proper spirit," he rebuked her sternly.

She slid along the seat until she was sitting close to him. She latched the center seat belt across her lap and then laid a slender hand atop the strong muscles of his thigh, feeling them contract reflexively beneath her light touch. She gazed up at him calmly. "You'll find me most eager to ensure that my first abduction is carried off in proper form. Just what do you consider is the appropriate spirit?" she asked huskily.

"Meek?" Cane mused aloud. "No, that's asking too much," he decided regretfully. "I suppose we'll just have to settle for respectful. Can you handle that?" He looked down at her questioningly.

Brianna traced a looping pattern across the top of his thigh with a pointed forefinger while she considered the matter earnestly. "You want me to *respect* you?" she murmured through quivering lips. She favored him with a mischievous smile and then assured him gravely, "Of course I'll always respect you, Cane, and your reputation is safe with me. I never kiss and tell."

Cane laughed. "Sweetheart, when I kiss you, you won't need to *tell*!" he promised softly.

Five

"I won't need to *tell*?" Brianna obediently fed Cane the straight line he was waiting for.

"No," he said with calm assurance. He half turned in the seat, tilted her face into position with a gentle hand beneath her chin and proceeded to demonstrate his point.

As first kisses go, it rated high on every scale except duration. Brianna would have been perfectly happy to sit in Cane's truck, parked in front of her parents' house, for several more hours, kissing and being kissed by Cane.

He didn't rush into intimacy. They had all the time in the world and Cane was in no hurry. His mouth moved questingly across the soft surface of Brianna's lips, tasting, tracing the tender margins of her mouth, postponing his inevitable acceptance of the invitation to deeper intimacy offered by her slightly parted lips.

Brianna slid her hand searchingly across the warm wall of Cane's chest, delighting in the strong rhythmic surge of his heartbeat beneath her flattened palm as she traced a broad path upward to find the heated vulnerability of his tanned throat. She slid her fingers beneath the open collar of his shirt, curving them around the side of his neck, savoring the fluid motion of muscles and tendons flexing beneath the skin as he tilted his head to allow her seeking hand greater freedom of movement.

"Mmmm."

Was that her throaty murmur of pleasure or his? Brianna neither knew nor cared. Now she knew why cats purred. She wanted to twine around Cane in a sinuous, boneless flow of muscle and skin, to wreathe around him like the never ending, upward spiral of the stripes on a barber pole, rising up and up into an increasing whirl of sensation and pleasure. No previous challenge she had ever accepted, no wild adventure she had formerly enjoyed could supply the heady excitement of this experience she shared with Cane.

By the time he drew away, trailing his strong fingers along the curve of her jaw, lifting his mouth from hers, still without initiating that deeper invasion, Brianna had learned a lesson in passion . . . and patience.

"Softly, slowly, Brianna beloved," Cane murmured soothingly as she lifted her face toward his again, blindly seeking, silently demanding that he not withold the bright magic of his kiss. "Not here, not now. Open your eyes, Bree," he commanded her huskily, urgently.

Obedient to the soft dictate, she lifted her heavy eyelids to reveal the drowsy glow of her green eyes. "Oh God, Brianna," Cane groaned. "Don't look at me like that or we'll never get to the restaurant for dinner." He laughed, a brief, shaken crack of sound. "We might not even make it out of your parents' front yard if we don't stop now," he warned when she seemed reluctant to heed his not altogether jesting admonition.

Mischief slowly replaced the sensual lethargy in Brianna's gaze. She breathed in and out once, deeply, with a sigh which came up from her toes. Then she smiled at him with a warm touch of sweet mockery. "Spoilsport," she drawled. "Are you afraid of my daddy's big, double-barreled shotgun?"

"Nope," Cane denied laconically. "Are you?"

"Nope," she replied, matching his brevity. "*I* know where he keeps the shells for it."

Cane threw back his head and laughed richly. "Oh, Brianna! You delightful brat!"

"If I'm a brat, what does that make you? A cradle robber?" she shot back smartly.

He leaned toward her, dropped a kiss on her forehead and said in a caressing tone, "That makes me a man who knows when he'd better get his truck in gear and on the road for town."

He adjusted and latched his seat belt. When he stretched out his hand to turn the ignition key, Brianna regretfully recognized that this delightful interlude was really over. But, she brightened, there was always the goodnight kiss to look forward to. A wicked smile curved the corners of her mouth. And who knew what else might transpire before they came to the goodnight kiss?

As Cane swung the truck in a tight circle to head it out on the track toward town, Brianna asked politely, "May I borrow the mirror?" and at his automatic assent, twisted the rearview mirror around so that she could see herself in it.

Cane had been right, she admitted silently as she inspected her reflection. She wouldn't have to *tell* anyone that she had been kissed. The cat who got the cream had nothing on her. She looked almost indecently self-satisfied. If just Cane's *kiss* could do this to her . . . Perhaps she would have to hide her father's shotgun shells after all.

She reapplied lip gloss, fluffed her dark hair into something approximating her original hairstyle and twisted the mirror back so Cane could readjust it to his satisfaction. He did so and after his hand returned to the steering wheel, she moved closer to his side, not so near that she interfered with his driving, but close enough so that their shoulders and thighs brushed companionably with each motion of the truck. She wasn't averse to speaking a little body language herself from time to time, when the situation required it. Some things were more pleasurably demonstrated than spoken.

At first there wasn't much conversation exchanged at the level of words as Cane guided the truck onto the road leading into town. He tuned the FM to an easy-listening station and Brianna was content to lean back and allow the residue of crackling sensual tension, which had flared so exquisitely between them, to drain away while the smooth strains of melody flowed gently, soothingly, around her. Their awareness of each other was still potent—it had been a force to be reckoned with from the first moment their eyes met in silent recognition on the front porch of Brianna's home—

but for the moment, neither the time nor the place were right.

"*Patience is a virtue, patience is a virtue,*" Brianna repeated silently. "*All things come to her who waits,*" she further reassured herself. Then Cane's hand dropped down from the steering wheel to catch and clasp her hand where it waited— patiently—in her lap. Almost absentmindedly his thumb began to stroke caressingly back and forth across the side of her laxly curled forefinger.

"*What do you know?*" Brianna marveled with smug enjoyment. "*Those old saws are right!*" With a contented sigh she nestled a fraction closer to Cane and then cast around in her mind for an innocuous subject to stimulate the conversation.

"I notice that your truck has four-wheel capability. Do you do much off-road recreational driving?" she asked curiously. It would be a pleasant bonus to discover that they shared at least some of the same enthusiasms.

"When I get the chance," he responded, picking up his cue amiably. "I have a camper shell that I use whenever I need extra security for equipment or material that I'm hauling in the truck, or when I go camping for extended periods of time. And of course the four-wheel capability is an absolute necessity for some on-site inspections when you really have to get back in the boonies. I also like to backpack into a wilderness area whenever I can manage a week or two of free time. I suppose," he continued thoughtfully, warming to his subject, "that I chose a career in construction engineering partly because of the opportunity it offered for outdoor work. I'd hate being cooped up in an office for most of the day. There's still a certain amount of office work necessary on an operation of this kind, but my partners take care of the majority of it. You'll like my partners," he added. "They're both married."

"Wouldn't I like them if they weren't married?" she teased.

"You wouldn't get the chance," he declared decisively. "I've known them for years and they were both born with an eye for quality and a predatory nature to match. My older sister tamed one and a cousin clipped the wings of the other so I guess it's safe to let Bob and Scott get a look at you. It might cause bad feelings in the family if I were forced to challenge either one to a duel," he concluded as though he had had to soberly assess the possibility.

Brianna said in a slightly stifled voice, "Oh, I would hate to be responsible for the revival of the Code Duello. You have such an . . . intriguing . . . style of compliment," she praised him demurely. "So . . ." She struggled for the appropriate word.

"Possessive?" he supplied easily.

"Precisely," she agreed promptly and then abandoned the struggle for sobriety. "Oh, Cane," she reproached mirthfully, "you make my side hurt from laughing." *"Would he gallantly offer to kiss it and make it well?"* she wondered hopefully. *"After all, 'Turn about et cetera.'"*

She had never laughed so comfortably with another man, she realized contentedly. Had never *liked* another man so well, so immediately, nor ever experienced the almost eerie empathy of interests and attitudes. She and Cane seemed to "match" in so many ways that she might, after all, become a convert to belief in Fate.

Brianna had always taken masculine attention for granted. She had been pampered, surrounded by love, from the moment of birth and only her mother's determined discipline and sedate good sense, plus her own innate self-sufficiency, had preserved her from the harmful effects of a doting father and an excessively fond—until she started leading where he had to follow—older brother. As she grew older, her circle of admirers expanded, but there weren't many fights over who would get to carry her books. She was too independent. She insisted on carrying her own books. Besides, her brother was always available to lighten or totally relieve her of the load whenever her childish strength began to flag along the two-mile track from the school bus stop to the ranch house door. They had trudged it every weekday unless the inclemency of the weather brought either Adam or Mary in the truck to meet them at the paved road, sparing them the effects of the wind and the soaking rain.

Brianna liked people, as individuals. Her infectious enthusiasm for life and her naturally warm-hearted nature ensured an abiding popularity with both sexes. If her female friends were wont to bewail her sturdy disinclination to make the most of her opportunities for romance, they were also quick to recognize that, in spite of her invariably off-hand response to persistent advances—she treated each of her swains the same, like brothers—she was still where the boys were. Brianna was the bait, but her delighted girlfriends were the wily anglers who trolled and then eventually landed the fish.

Because she was high-spirited and seemingly

extroverted, few had recognized the quiet core of solitary autonomy she protected so instinctively and diligently. Brianna would laugh with her friends, lead them into—and out of—mischief, commiserate with and console them, share food and finances, but she had never shared the private, intensely personal complex of thoughts, dreams, beliefs and fears which defined and distinguished the quintessential Brianna.

Her family, who loved her and were loved by her, had long ago acknowledged the existence and essential privacy of that final intimate kingdom of the mind. They had recognized and respected her occasional mental and physical retreat into a solitude where no one had ever been invited to intrude. Both of her parents possessed a deep, fundamental regard for the franchise of individuality and had raised their children to respect, and not abuse, that freedom. Brianna might go away, but she always came back, refreshed, renewed and eager to reenter the flow of family life.

Now, for the first time in her life, Brianna was impelled by an irresistible desire to breach the barrier of her solitude and invite another human being—Cane, only Cane—to enter the sanctuary of her secret thoughts. Joyously, recklessly, with an endearingly blithe disregard for possible consequences, she was planning to do a graceful swan dive headfirst into the deep, invigorating waters of passionate commitment.

Cane, as yet unaware of the gist of Brianna's momentous resolutions, drove calmly and steadily to the restaurant he had previously chosen with gluttony aforethought. He parked the truck smoothly, got out and then proceeded to do the gentlemanly thing, i.e., politely assist Brianna to descend from the truck's high seat. Keeping in mind their mutual tendency to utilize opportunities, whether fleeting or not, he contrived, with Brianna's admittedly enthusiastic cooperation, to slide her sensuously down against the muscular length of his body in the process of getting her safely to earth.

Brianna briefly regretted her lamentable lack of foresight. Why hadn't she thought to leave her purse in the truck so she could climb back up to get it and thus be forced to ask Cane's help to alight once again? Well, she'd know better next time, she vowed. Her mama hadn't raised a slow learner.

Cane laid his arm around the back of her shoulders and Brianna slid her arm across the back of his lean waist. As they strode toward the entrance of the restaurant, she playfully walked her fingers up and down his side, "counting his ribs" with the deliberate intention of discovering whether or not he was ticklish. He was. But he also possessed enormous self-control. After his initial involuntary jump, he held himself stiffly, set his jaw firmly, and endured. None of her subsequent probes elicited the slightest flinch, but he did incline his head toward her and murmur ominously, "Everyone has an Achilles heel, Brianna Elizabeth. Shall I take the time to find yours?"

Brianna gulped. The arch of her foot was lethally sensitive. Grass blades or lightly stroking fingers had been known to drive her to the brink, and over, of raving giggledom. Alex and Drew were both fully aware of that particular unfortunate affliction, having gleefully, and unfairly, exploited it on occasions when they managed to pin her down during impromptu wrestling matches on the family room floor. But it always took 'two of them! For a suitable reward—actually, all Cane would have to do was ask them; neither of her brothers possessed a speck of loyalty!—they'd treacherously betray every single weak spot in her defenses that they had discovered during their years of being her brothers.

She immediately quit poking at his side and initiated what she hoped he would interpret as a sensuous massage of the hard muscles covering the side of his rib cage. He leaned into the kneading pressure of her supple fingers and rumbled with pleasure, deep in his throat. "Ummm. Very nice," he rumbled. She relaxed. "But not nice enough." She stiffened. "You'll have to placate me further. Later."

She relaxed again. "Fair enough," she assented happily, already planning how best to . . . placate . . . him.

He released her, opened the restaurant door and indicated that she should precede him. Once inside he caught her hand in his as they paused patiently for the aloof indifference of the hostess to relax enough to acknowledge their presence. Her distant demeanor warmed perceptibly after her glance swept over Cane's broad shoulders and strong-boned face, but it thawed dramatically when her recognition extended to the woman who stood quietly at his side.

"Brianna Graeme! When did you get back into town?" the lacquered beauty questioned loudly, but with every evidence of genuine pleasure. "Does Carl know that you're home?"

Brianna winced slightly. "I got home yesterday, Margo, and no, I don't believe Carl knows I'm home," she answered the questions in sequence. She deliberately moved closer to Cane and tilted her head to brush against his arm. She emphasized the message with an unmistakable look of adoration up at Cane's wryly resigned face.

"Oh." Margo had obviously received and correctly interpreted Brianna's message. "I . . . I'll tell Carl I saw you," she said sadly. "Would you come this way? Your table . . . your reservation . . . ?" she stuttered in a flustered garble.

"The reservation is in the name of Taylor," Cane offered helpfully, his expression remaining impressively bland.

"I'll tell Carl," the older woman repeated involuntarily. "I mean, your table is ready, Mr. Taylor."

She led them to a choice table for two, twitched the linen table cloth to straighten an infinitesimal wrinkle, murmured "Nice to see you again, Brianna. I hope you enjoy your meal, Brianna, Mr. Taylor. Your waitress will be with you in a moment," and left them abruptly.

"Going to tell Carl?" Cane wondered whimsically.

"Carl is her considerably younger brother," Brianna explained as she sank into the chair Cane held for her. "He lives with Margo and her husband and their four children. She's getting desperate to marry him off and transfer his appetite and his laundry over to some other woman's stove and washing machine, and she's not too particular about which candidate is elected for the job. I've known Carl since grade school. He has sweaty palms," she finished, dismissing the hapless Carl succinctly.

"How did you find out about his palms?" Cane asked sternly and deliberately as he took his seat across from her.

"Mandatory ballroom dancing classes in junior high P.E.," she replied with virtuous composure.

Suddenly various people began to converge on the table. A busboy filled their goblets with ice water and supplied them with a napkin-shrouded wicker basket of hot bread accompanied by a chilled saucer bearing a pyramid of foil-wrapped pats of butter. The cocktail waitress took their order for aperitifs and then swayed away to flirt with the bartender while he made up their drinks. Their dinner waitress presented imposing menus and discreetly withdrew until they indicated that they were ready to make their selections.

After the temporary bustle had died away, Cane asked straight-faced, "Is the service always this . . . attentive?"

"Not that I've noticed." Brianna shook her head. "It must be your blue eyes. But the food *is* good and their servings are exceedingly generous. I believe that was a requirement," she said lightly.

"That's right." Cane matched her light tone. "I believe in taking every advantage I can get."

Brianna could see that they were knee-deep in the water already and, judging by the bold gleam in Cane's eyes, he was perfectly willing to lead her in over her verbal head. She wanted to learn to swim, but she didn't plan to have her first lesson in a public restaurant!

She changed the subject. Cane's eyes narrowed with amused comprehension and she wrinkled her nose at him reprovingly, but he accepted the new direction of the conversation meekly enough.

She didn't deceive herself that he would *always* be this tractable. No one who had met Cane Taylor would ever make the mistake of believing he was a man who could be easily led. He might be easygoing, but he was in no sense of the term biddable. She wasn't really a particular student of physiognomy but no man with a jawline like Cane's could be anything but stubborn when the notion took him.

The service continued to be good, the food was, as expected, sumptuous and except for two trifling incidents, the meal proceeded smoothly. Cane's equanimity was tested but not sorely tried on those occasions, when several enterprising male diners spotted Brianna and came over to welcome her home and to ask how long she would be staying this time. He accepted each rather chilly acknowledgment of Brianna's introduction of him with grave courtesy and unimpaired urbanity, but Brianna apprehensively noted a disturbing gleam of mocking humor shining deep in his eyes. She suddenly had the sinking feeling that her brothers and her father might not be the only ones whose teasing she had to deal with, and Cane's dry sense of humor might be all the harder to counter for being so deceptively understated.

After the second visitor to the table had come and gone, Cane asked mildly, "Did your former escorts always have to run this same type of gauntlet when they took you out?"

Brianna didn't miss his deliberate emphasis of the past tense and she smiled before she answered sweetly, "Actually, no, but then, you see, they all knew each other already and had pretty well written each other off as effective competition." She could only hope that the strategy of a frontal attack would work as effectively against Cane's teasing as it had against her brothers'.

Cane grinned broadly and said with deep satisfaction, "That's fine, just fine."

Brianna stared at him in puzzlement. Just what kind of a reaction was that supposed to be?

With a look of cool determination, Cane captured her hand and raised it to his mouth in a slow, deliberate gesture so that everyone in the restaurant could watch, if they felt so inclined. He placed an ostentatious kiss in her palm, folded her hand around it and laid her hand gently down again. "There. That should take care of it," he said decisively. "The 'competition' is officially closed. I've just declared myself the winner."

What could she say? Nothing.

What could she do? Laugh!

So she laughed, a happy ripple of pure enjoyment and pleasure, expressing her delight with life in general and Cane in particular. After they had finished their dessert and Cane had settled the bill, she slid deftly beneath the protective, possessive weight of his arm and wrapped her own arm securely around his waist before they made their exit. When one is making a statement, one might as well do a thorough job of it.

As they strolled slowly toward the truck through the balmy evening air, Brianna savored that special sense of pleasant satisfaction which meant that she had just dined exceedingly well but not to unpleasant excess. She was also deliciously conscious of the smooth coordination of Cane's muscles as he walked beside her, effortlessly adjusting the length and rhythm of his greater stride to her shorter step. Everything about this man pleasured her. His tall, strong body appealed directly to the specific sexual instincts which had always been inherent, but dormant, in her strongly sensual nature. No other man had succeeded in rousing those impulses to urgent and demanding awareness but, with Cane, she was ardent and eager to experience all delights possible in an intimate sharing of the physical body. She appreciated his dry but wicked sense of humor and basked in the warmth of his slow smile. The calm competence of his manner told her he was a man to trust, a man to ride a wild river with, but, above all else, he was *her* man. She could not explain it—it had hit her like a thunderbolt, the classic French *coup de foudre*—but she was certainly going to enjoy it!

In spite of the amount of food she had just consumed, Cane didn't seem to notice any significant increase in her weight because, with the deft assistance of his helpful hands, she flew up to the high seat of the truck just as lightly as she had before. While she settled comfortably and waited for him to walk around to the driver's side, she considered briefly just what that small courtesy revealed and confirmed about him. Of course it showed that he liked to touch her—his hands were silently eloquent whenever and wherever they lingered on her body—but of equal importance, it also demonstrated that he was constantly conscious of her injured state and was evidently determined to make sure that she didn't damage herself further by attempting physical feats which might stress or strain her battered body. Both times when he had boosted her up into the truck, he had carefully placed his hands to avoid putting any pressure on her bruised side and his smooth straight lift had ensured that she neither twisted nor pulled at the wrenched muscles. Small silent actions, but they were touchingly expressive of his concern and tender solicitude. Brianna was conscious of a sweet inner warmth which had nothing at all to do with the temperature of the evening air.

When Cane climbed into the truck, he didn't start the engine immediately. Instead he leaned back and slid his arm along the top of the seat behind Brianna's shoulders, but his fingers didn't attempt to bridge the small distance to touch her. His face was soberly thoughtful and his eyes were softly serious as they scanned her trustfully upturned face.

"Where now, Brianna?" His deep voice was quiet and grave.

"Where now?" she repeated with brief confusion.

"Where would you like to go now?" he clarified. "Would you like to find some place where we can have a drink and perhaps dance?"

Suddenly she understood. It was up to her to set the pace. They both knew what they wanted, what was inevitable, but Cane was letting her know that *she* would be the one to say "when." Brianna didn't hesitate. Her decision had been made from the moment she had first set eyes on Cane and all that was left was to ratify it in his arms.

"Some place where we can drink and dance," she repeated expressionlessly, as though academically considering a list of suitable establishments.

No slow smile Cane had yet given her could

match the deliberate deviltry of the teasing tilt and curve of Brianna's beautiful mouth. Cane involuntarily sucked in a deep, shaky breath. "Do you happen to have a stereo or a radio at your apartment?" she questioned huskily and then continued informatively, "I like white wine. There are lots of stores around here that carry a varied selection of wines and some of them are open all night."

Demurely she waited for Cane's reaction.

"I think I know the perfect place," he said, picking up his cue promptly. "It's very exclusive, but I happen to be a personal friend of the owner. It has soft music and even softer lights and a small but adequate wine cellar. Does it sound like a place you'd like?"

"If you recommend it, I'm sure I'll be . . . satisfied," she responded smoothly. Her expression had all the guileless innocence of an apprentice angel. But Lucifer was an angel too, before The Fall.

Cane's searching stare was sharply suspicious but Brianna stared right back at him with bland naïveté. Innuendo? Double entendre? Nonsense. He must be hearing things!

"And the Devil can quote scripture with a straight face too," Cane muttered dryly, obviously convinced that he had heard what he had heard.

"I beg your pardon?" Brianna responded primly, but her façade of conscious propriety was slipping. Butter might not melt in her mouth but there were canary feathers and cream all over her chin.

"Your halo just fell down over your eyes," Cane advised helpfully.

"The better to see you through, Grandpa," she retorted.

"Don't look at me through a rose-colored halo, Brianna," Cane instructed quietly, momentarily serious. "I'm just a man." He started the truck and drove it out of the parking lot.

Brianna snuggled closer to him. "'Just' isn't precisely the word I'd choose to describe you," she said, playing with the word idly, "although if you equate 'just' with 'only,' I'll agree that you're my only man. Or if you prefer to use 'just' in the sense of 'fair' I will also agree that you are 'fair' according to a number of definitions of the word, such as 'pleasing to the eye' and 'light; blond as opposed to brunet' or perhaps 'characterized by honesty; civil or courteous in manner.' I might even allow 'objective' although I'm afraid I'd have to disallow 'dispassionate' . . ."

"Brianna, either your mother swallowed a dictionary while she was pregnant with you or she fed you too much alphabet soup when you were a child." Cane's voice shook with laughter as he negotiated a turn.

"My father once said my mind was like a sponge, that I just soaked up words," she informed him airily, her eyes sparkling with relish of the word-play.

"Are you sure he wasn't referring to the fact that a sponge is full of holes?" Cane teased as he steered the truck into a covered, numbered parking space in the tenants' parking section of an attractive apartment complex.

"I take back 'civil or courteous in manner'!" she yelped in mock indignation. "'Average' and 'mediocre' are also accepted definitions of 'fair,' you know, as in: 'His intelligence and his sense of humor were only fair.'"

Cane laughed heartily. "So the pedant can bite back," he observed lightly.

"Of course," she responded, feigning haughtiness. "Haven't you ever heard the phrase 'a ferocious pedant' before? In fact"—her voice dropped confidingly—"I always post a sign, BEWARE THE PEDANT, on my trailer door when I'm working and don't want to be disturbed. That way, by the time the door-to-door salesman, or whoever it is, has checked with a dictionary to discover that a pedant isn't a person with a dangerous foot fetish, I've had time to finish my work and am long gone."

Cane was still chuckling as he helped her down from the truck. Brianna wrapped the warmth of his laughter around her heart and slid gracefully into his waiting arms. They closed around her gently but with a distinctly possessive strength and she snuggled cooperatively against him, demonstrating a regrettably deliberate intent to entice. Cane responded with immediate and gratifying enthusiasm, holding her closely against his body for a timeless moment before he sighed heavily and reluctantly eased his firm embrace. She leaned back slightly in the loosened circle of his arms and cocked her head inquiringly, silently asking why he had called a halt. Wasn't he going to kiss her?

There was a distinctly wry twist to his mouth when he answered her unspoken question. "We can't stay out here any longer, Brianna."

With her overdeveloped penchant for living dangerously, she had no thought of leaving well enough alone. "Why not?" she breathed in a teasingly seductive tone. "I thought we were doing just fine."

It was amazing how adept she was becoming at this, considering how little practice she'd had at it before. Brianna congratulated herself complacently. It just went to prove that a girl could always depend on Ma Nature and instinct when experience wasn't available! Flirting—with Cane—had turned out to be a highly enjoyable pastime and she fully intended to make up for all the time she had lost due to her previous lack of interest in the sport.

Cane's voice was stern but his grin was undeniably sensual. "We can't stay here," he explained carefully, "because of a certain clause in the fine print of the lease I signed when I moved into my apartment. The covenants of this apartment complex strictly and specifically forbid any tenant to indulge in lascivious advances, let alone make mad passionate love, in the middle of this rather public parking lot and, my delicious torment, if we stay here any longer like this"—he ran an expressive hand from her shoulders down to her hips, pressing her against his body briefly—"that's exactly what is going to happen to you on this very spot. You deliberately do dreadful things to my self-control and you're enjoying every moment of it, aren't you?" he accused her with humorously plaintive resignation.

Brianna resolutely ignored the blush that heated her cheeks and admitted shamelessly, "I certainly am enjoying it. Aren't you?"

"You'd be worth getting evicted for," Cane assured her chivalrously, "but I did promise you cool wine, soft music and . . ." he paused suggestively, "dancing. Shall we go?"

"You lead, I'll follow," Brianna quipped.

He groaned. "Does it just come naturally to you?" he asked ruefully as he guided her toward his apartment.

"Does what come naturally?" She tried hard to look uncomprehending.

"Making bad puns," he said succinctly.

"All puns, by definition, must be bad," she informed him serenely. "If they don't make you want to groan, then they haven't been done correctly. My ability was a gift bestowed upon me in my cradle," she said modestly, "by a slightly wacky fairy godmother, and I have labored tirelessly for many years to raise my facility for words to its present low level. If you think *I* have a talent, though, you ought to hear my mother after she's had a couple of glasses of wine. My whole family has been known to resort to sign language to avoid giving her an opening for a pun when she's really on a hot streak."

Cane stopped before a door and fished in his pocket for a keycase. As he inserted the key, he glanced down at her and said consolingly, "Well, these aberrations show up at times in the nicest families. Someday I'll have to tell you about my great-uncle Arthur." He pushed the door open and stepped aside to allow her to enter his apartment.

Without the slightest discernible hesitation, Brianna stepped across the threshold.

Six

Cane's apartment decor could best be described as Spartan Luxury, Spartan because there was very little furniture and Luxury because what there was, was luxurious. She walked through a small entry hall into a thickly carpeted living room, which contained a matching couch and chair upholstered in rich suedecloth, several hanging lamps, and an entertainment center consisting of a video monitor, a VCR unit and a stereo/cassette unit with large—and, she thought, probably very expensively efficient—speakers precisely arranged to ensure full and resonant fidelity. Three oil paintings, one of which she recognized as a Talbot, hung on the walls. The only incongruous note was a shabby leather ottoman, positioned in front of the couch at just the right distance for Cane to comfortably prop his feet while watching TV or reading. A pile of periodicals and newspapers teetered in an unstable tower beside one end of the couch.

"The hassock, the paintings, the books and the

electronic hardware I brought with me," Cane explained, waving an expressive hand to encompass the contents of the room, "but I bought all the furniture—what there is of it—when I moved in here. This is the first time I knew for sure that I was going to be in one place for more than a year. In the past I've always rented furnished apartments, but I finally got tired of sleeping in beds that were too small and too soft and being surrounded by apartment-blah color schemes. So this time I decided to start with at least the bare minimums and"—he smiled slightly sheepishly— "I'm afraid that bare minimum is all that you'll find in the kitchen. Will you mind drinking your wine out of regular glasses instead of wine goblets?"

"Not at all," Brianna said absently. "Books, what books?" she asked curiously, since there was no reading matter visible except for the tipsy pile of periodicals leaning against the end of the couch. Did Cane read for entertainment and if so, what genres did he favor? She herself was a voracious reader and always left a trail of paperbacks behind her wherever she traveled, donated to the nearest local library when she moved on because of the space limitations of the trailer.

"In the second bedroom, first door to your left down the hall," he directed as he walked into the kitchen. "That's the office/library/catch-all room."

Cane seemed to have a wide-ranging taste in recreational reading. Science fiction, mysteries and a respectable scattering of biographies and nonfiction shared the adequate but unglamorous shelving of pine boards and bricks which lined one wall of the extra bedroom. Technical manuals, journals and reference books were given somewhat more sophisticated accommodations, on bookshelves flanking a broad flat desk which supported a mug full of pencils and pens, a reading lamp, a scatter of manila folders and a home computer with printer. A utilitarian metal filing cabinet, an equally utilitarian swivel chair and three cardboard boxes completed the room's furnishings.

Brianna swept a considering eye over the room. There was a lot of scope for the woman's touch, but it was going to take a heck of a lot more than a few throw pillows and a couple of vases of flowers.

When she wandered back into the living room, the wine, the music and the soft lights were all waiting for her. And so was Cane. He handed her a glass of wine, waited unhurriedly while she took a sip and smiled her approval of his selection, then gently plucked the glass from her hand and set it beside his own atop the ottoman, which he had shoved back out of the way. "Kick off your shoes," he invited as he held out his arms. "I promise I won't demolish your toes."

He had already slipped out of his own shoes and stood now in his sock feet, waiting patiently for her to come to him. She kicked her shoes aside and, with a graceful motion reminiscent of a bird eagerly reaching the aerie at the end of a long, lonely journey, Brianna glided into his open arms. They closed around her with the swift spring of a lover's ambush and the falcon was captured, held close against his heart, snared in the tender net fashioned from her own desires and dreams. Slowly, almost imperceptibly at first, they began to dance, responding fluidly to the compelling cadence of the soft music from the stereo.

Brianna's hands slid up over Cane's chest, palms

flattened and fingers spread as they stroked a wide, blind path upward, cresting the broad slope of his shoulders to shape themselves around the warm column of his neck, slipping finger-deep into the soft, thick hair that curved to the contour of his skull. While her hands were traveling upward, Cane's hands moved down, outlining the smooth incurve of her waist, traversing the gentle flare of her hips, spreading out below the back of her waist to guide her through the steps of the dance with the subtle pressure of his hands and body. He led and Brianna followed, anticipating and responding so smoothly to each movement of his body that they might well have shared a single network of nerves and neurons, for the activating impulses seemed to travel simultaneously through both of their bodies.

Eyes closed, she rested her head against Cane's shoulder, the better to savor every sweet new intimacy: the firm pressure of his chest against her breasts, each recurrent brush of his thighs against her own, the warm weight of his hands splayed over her hips. They were the promise, the sure prelude to the final intimacy. With a sigh of deep content she nestled closer, wordlessly endorsing the immemorial feminine invitation to her chosen man.

Slowly, as though in leisurely acceptance of her invitation, Cane's hands began to stroke up the line of her spine and across her back, stopping just below the level of her shoulder blades. As his hands spanned over the sides of her rib cage, he exerted a gentle pressure to flex her upper body back and slightly away from his chest. Brianna was quick to cooperate. She lifted her head and slid her hands down to rest atop his shoulders, at the same time arching her back slightly, which had the interesting side effect of pressing her hips more firmly against Cane's lower body. It made it difficult to dance but by that time they had forgotten about the music anyway and were now listening to an entirely different drummer, who was doing really crazy things with the tempo of their heartbeats.

Brianna tilted her face up toward Cane's, letting her eyelids drift closed to capture and keep the reflection of his strong face in the clear depths of her eyes. There was no mistake. This time he was really going to *kiss* her!

His long fingers cupped the sides of her breasts and his palms pressed upward lightly, accepting the weight of the firm curves while his mouth searched for, and found, the eager welcome of her parted lips. Their breaths mingled, a brief preliminary to intimacy, before Cane's mouth initiated the gentle invasion Brianna had wanted, had been waiting for, from the first moment she had seen him. Patience was often a sometime thing with her and the ardent intimacy of his deep kiss was a delightful indication that now she no longer had to continue to practice that singularly boring virtue!

On more than one occasion in the past, certain frustrated and disgruntled suitors had suggested that she might derive considerable benefit from a course of therapy designed to correct a terminal case of frigidity. Ha! Fat lot they knew! She had just been waiting. But she didn't have to wait any longer.

She began to move sinuously against him, responding deliberately to the heady erotic stimulus of his caressing hands and persuasive lips, intuitively matching the langorously twining rhythm of his intimate invasion of her mouth. An involuntary, wordless croon vibrated somewhere in the depths of her throat, a barely audible thrum of need and encouragement which was felt in the bones more than heard by the ears. With urgent eloquence, she spoke the primal language of the senses, which has and needs no words and yet is utterly comprehensible.

Slowly, Cane ended the deep kiss and then pressed the side of his cheek against her temple. His hands slid from her breasts around to her back, pulling her tightly against the full length of his body in an almost agonized reflex silently and poignantly expressive of his need. He wanted her. She knew it. She could *feel* the urgency of his desire as he held her in the taut circle of his arms. Encouragingly, she snuggled as close to him as she could get—given the inconvenient fact that they were dressed in clothes which were suddenly entirely too bulky and restrictive! As he held her, Cane rocked gently, a subtle swaying motion that somehow soothed even while it heightened her awareness of the exquisite pleasure potentials inherent in the human body.

"Oh, Brianna, I've been looking for you all my life," he said deeply, earnestly, his voice ragged with emotion. "I love you. You know that, don't you? Cupid isn't some funny, fat little boy who goes around shooting tiny darts into people. He's really a giant who swings a sledgehammer with devastating power and he hit me right between the eyes the first time I saw you, as you stood in your parents' front yard. After you had hugged and kissed your family, you started walking toward me. I wanted you to walk straight into my arms. You didn't even know I existed, but you were coming straight toward me and I knew by the time you reached me that I wasn't ever going to let you walk away."

Brianna tilted her head so that she could see his face and read his expression. The absolute tenderness in his voice, the stark sincerity of his measured words, affected her powerfully. Cane was a man who wasn't ashamed to say what he felt, a man who meant exactly what he said. He had said it. He meant it. He loved her!

But she had known that. Always.

For her, standing in the shadowed shelter of the porch of her parents' home, it had been a sense of glad recognition, that sudden stunning realization: *Oh! Here you are at last! I've been waiting for you.* Not, perhaps, as *physical* as a sledgehammer blow between the eyes, but just as effective, just as certain.

Brianna lifted her hands from his shoulders and carefully framed his face between her warm palms. She smiled at him with the same heart-stoppingly radiant smile that had illuminated her face on that first day—was it really only yesterday? Choosing her words deliberately, with precision, she responded soberly to his words. "I love you, Cane. I will never walk away from you. I have waited for you." Those three simple sentences conveyed everything, the totality of her commitment. Brianna never did things by halves.

Then Cane bent his head and kissed her and she discovered that he didn't intend to do things by halves either! He swept the tip of his tongue across the soft surface of her lips, probing, parting them with a light but insistent pressure to again permit his possessive exploration of her mouth. His hands began to move questingly over her torso, restlessly investigating the firm contours of the figure so tantalizingly veiled by the thin fabric of her dress.

Brianna was much more direct. She slid her hands down from where they had framed his face, at the same time exerting a gentle, deliberate pressure against his chest with her elbows until he yielded just enough to enable her to slide her arms down, under and around his back at waist level. The purpose of this deftly performed maneuver quickly became apparent when her busy fingers tugged the tail of his shirt out of the waistband of his slacks and slipped beneath the fabric to begin an exploration of the taut skin covering the layered muscles of his back. Kneading lightly as she went, like a kitten with sheathed claws, she walked her fingers slowly up on either side of his spine as far as she could comfortably reach, to spread her hands, palms flat, fingers wide, just below his shoulder blades. With the silent, secret language of the body, she communicated the depth of her longing, expressed her pleasure in the sensuous contact of skin to bare skin. She slid her hands and forearms caressingly across the broad expanse of his back, testing with sensitive fingertips the texture and tone of the sleek musculature.

Somewhere below her left ear, Cane was tasting the soft skin at the side of her throat. She heard him mutter thickly, "You really don't want any more wine, do you, sweetheart?"

Although she had the feeling that it had been a purely rhetorical question, Brianna managed to whisper a stifled "No."

"And you don't want to dance any more either, do you?"

This time she *knew* it was a rhetorical question because, even as he spoke, Cane scooped her up into his arms and started walking toward the hall leading to the bedrooms and bathroom—and she didn't think that he was heading toward the bathroom to give them both a cold shower!

A shower, cold or otherwise, was evidently the farthest thing from his mind. Cane shouldered the bedroom door wide, carried Brianna over the threshold and flicked the light switch by the door with his elbow. Soft light bloomed from a bedside table lamp, illuminating only a portion of what looked like an acre of bed stretching away into the shadowy corners of the room.

At this particular moment, Brianna wasn't terribly interested in decor, but she did notice that Cane hadn't bothered to furnish himself with more than the uninspired necessities of bedding. Stark white sheets and pillowcases covered the mattress and pillows and a couple of dull gold thermal blankets were neatly folded and laid at the foot of the bed. She liked colored sheets. She would color coordinate Cane at her leisure. In the meantime there were much more urgent and interesting things to concentrate on.

Cane carried her over to the side of the bed and set her gently on her feet. With one hand he grasped the corner of the top sheet and flicked it toward the foot of the bed in a crisp billow of white. And now . . .

If she had bothered to think about it, Brianna might have expected to feel a certain amount of maidenly shyness. This was, after all, her first time—and how, by the by, was she to casually drop *that* particular tidbit of information into any preliminary conversation? But two factors intervened. The first was that the naked human body, masculine version thereof, was no mystery to her. How could it be? She had two brothers, neither of whom was noted for his particular sense of modesty within the family, both of whom slept in the raw and often wandered the halls of home in that natural state when going to and from the shower as the occasion arose and the mood struck them. Since their mother was known to frown ferociously upon damp towels left crumpled on the bedroom carpet, the mood generally dictated that they leave the wet towels hung more or less neatly on the towel rack in the bathroom serving their bedrooms. Modesty was simply not worth the extra effort, involving as it did a second trip to the bathroom just to return a towel! Alex and Drew both firmly believed that energy conservation should begin at home.

The second and by far more important factor was simply, Brianna was not shy of Cane. She loved him. It seemed perfectly natural to share everything with him, including the deepest physical intimacy. There could be no shame in seeing herself reflected in the bright mirror of his eyes.

In the soft light and long shadows of the small lamp they began to undress—themselves and each other. Fingers that had buttoned and unbuttoned competently since post-toddlerhood suddenly began to display a disconcerting tendency to fumble—

Cane tossed his shirt to the floor minus a button. But Brianna, who possessed an adequate share of normal feminine foresight, had selected her dress for the evening with great deliberation. The one she wore had been designed with a minimum of buttons and a maximum of easy sliding zipper.

She dealt with the button at the neck above the zipper herself—she had observed the fate of Cane's shirt—but then presented her back to Cane with a trustful "Will you help me with my zipper, darling?"

"I think a woman must have invented buttons," Cane grumbled wryly as his fingers eased the zipper down its smooth track. He hadn't missed Brianna's brief spurt of amusement when the button flew off his shirt. "But"—his voice deepened and she felt the warmth of his breath at the nape of her neck—"I do believe a man was responsible for the invention of the zipper." As his hands slid the dress off her shoulders and down her arms, easing it carefully over her hips and releasing it to slide to the floor in a soft tangle of fabric around their feet, his warm lips began to press slow, tantalizing kisses into the curve of her neck and shoulder, lightly nipping small folds of skin between his lips, then savoring her special taste with slow sweeps of his tongue. Brianna shivered convulsively, her whole body quivering in a brief spasm of anticipation.

Her hands dealt deftly with the front closure of her bra, which then quickly followed the dress to the floor. Cane was swift to take advantage of the resultant enticing exposure. His arms pulled her back firmly against the broad support of his chest while his hands curved, cupped, around her breasts, creating an erotically exciting replacement for the bra she had so eagerly discarded.

"Brianna, Brianna . . ." His voice was thick and strained, each husky repetition of her name an eloquent expression of the depth of his feelings. "You fit into my hands as perfectly as you fit into my heart. I love you with my mind, little wild bird, but my body loves you too. Let me love you now."

While his deep voice whispered irresistible enticements in her ear, Cane's hands simultaneously and delicately performed their own potent brand of seductive magic. Using the tips of his forefingers, he traced slow circles around each dusky, silky soft areola, provocatively rubbing work-calloused fingers against the sides of her sweetly aching nipples, occasionally varying and enhancing the tantalizing stimulation by sweeping a light stroke directly across the exquisitely sensitized tip of each erect nipple. When he gently captured and rolled each swollen bud of tender flesh between careful thumb and forefinger, that spontaneous muted purr vibrated again in the depths of her throat and her back arched involuntarily, lifting her breasts in an unmistakable invitation.

As her spine arched, Brianna reached back to spread her hands, flat palmed, against the tense muscles of Cane's flanks, wordlessly encouraging him to press forward with intimate explicitness. The swift upward thrust of her breasts against the curve of his palms and the slow, instinctively rhythmic movement of her buttocks against his lower body wrenched a sharp groan from Cane, an inarticulate sound of imperative desire.

"Yes, Cane. Oh yes! Please. Please love me now," Brianna whispered demandingly.

If he didn't do something soon . . . Was it possible to *rape* a dilatory but otherwise willing man? She was sure that this excruciating frustration was doing dreadful things to the state of her health. Not to mention her sanity! Fleetingly she regretted her inexperience. Did one *always* feel such an irresistible compulsion to fling oneself against the object of one's desire and ravish him where he stood . . . or lay? A brief flicker of common sense scoffed "Nonsense!" If that were the case, ardent couples, passionately entwined in the most torrid and embarrassing of embraces, would continually litter the sidewalks and hallways.

Bah! Who cared about anyone else's frustrations? She wanted Cane and she wanted him *now!*

Cane's hands ranged slowly down the length of her body, temporarily abandoning the rich curves of her breasts with palpable reluctance, until they came to rest on her hip bones, just below the slender curve of her waist. Exerting a steady, gentle pressure, he turned Brianna to face him again. His right hand left her hip and stroked upward toward her throat, knuckles brushing deliberately against the full inner curve as his hand traversed the warm valley between her breasts, until it touched and tilted her chin, silently encouraging her eyes to meet his ardent gaze.

"Now, Brianna?"

Another rhetorical question. Brianna didn't waste time or words. She let the warm pressure of her breasts against his chest and the devouring intensity of her kiss answer for her. *Now, for heaven's sake. Now!*

She sensed, rather than heard, a soft rumble of laughter in Cane's chest—*could* he have read her mind?—but she didn't really care. He had the message now.

Were there only five primary senses? Brianna couldn't believe it. There had to be another one, the one that had transformed her whole body into a receptor of ecstatic sensation, a focus for exquisite pleasure . . . and knowledge. Now she knew Cane.

Perhaps it was a composite sense, a sum greater than its parts. It included sight, of course, the precious ability to visually appreciate the sleek symmetry of his lean and rangy body, so beautifully, arrogantly masculine, modeled from genetic clay by a master sculptor to create a living work of art. It was touch as well, to "see" with hands, using sensitive fingers to measure length, breadth, depth. His touch, her touch, their touch, the tactile pleasures of skin touching skin over bone, over hard muscle, over soft curves and in warm, secret places. Curves and hollows, skin like silk, skin rough with hair. Textures, smooth, raspy and sleek, sliding, pressing, the elemental contact, communication without words.

And when there were words? The sounds of love, whispered, muttered, moaned. Sighs, words to weave an incantation, a spell to bind a heart. Promises. Praise. Words that say "You are the first, the only, the ever." And when words fail, the soft cries flutter, take wing and then soar exultantly, fading slowly, softly to triumphant content.

Taste and scent, inextricably mingled, unique. Salty, musky, sweet honey and tangy herb. The special scent of man, wo-man, separate, blended.

"I love. He loves. We love." Brianna carefully tasted the flavor of the short declarative sentences

and found them absolutely delicious. With a langorous wiggle, she snuggled closer against Cane's left side and slid her hand up from his waist, across the hard muscles of his chest, tracking the steady beat of his heart until her hand came to rest just above the strong, rhythmic pulse. She relaxed, sleepily content, cradled in the possessive curve of his arm, her head resting on the sinewy pillow of his shoulder and upper chest, her left leg thrown in a slant across his hip and thigh and the toes of that foot tucked under the slightly flexed arch of his right knee, a picture of comfortable, trusting intimacy.

Her eyes were drifting shut when Cane said conversationally, "I think you'll like my parents. Is there room for them to stay out at the ranch or shall I make motel reservations for them? I don't know how many of my brothers and sisters and their families will be able to travel on such short notice, but as many as can, will come, and they can all stay at that new motel out on 680."

Brianna idly twirled several of the silky straight hairs on Cane's chest into a tangled knot and said cheerfully, without the slightest hesitation, "Of course your parents will stay at the ranch with my folks. There's a very comfortable guest room. That was almost the first thing Mom had drawn into the plans when she and Dad were designing the new ranch house, because Drew's arrival meant she didn't have an extra bedroom any more in the old house. It was always musical beds when company came, so a guest bedroom and bath had high priority in the new house."

She paused to consider. "Actually, depending on how many can come, we might be able to fit them all in at the ranch. We could shift Alex and Drew out to the trailer to sleep—it cools off here at night so much that a fan does a good job of making the trailer very comfortable—and that would free up two bedrooms. Kids could sleep on pallets out in the family room. It's been the site of many a slumber party in the past and we have a supply of thick foam rubber mats. I'm taking for granted nieces and nephews but there are some, aren't there?" She had found out a lot about Cane—hadn't she just!—but there hadn't been time for *everything*.

"Four. My older brother and my older sister each have two."

"Mmmm. And how many brothers and sisters all told, since we're on the subject of family?" Brianna asked curiously.

"One brother and sister older, one sister and brother younger," he enumerated obligingly. "I'm the man in the middle. But we weren't actually on the subject of family, except incidentally," he corrected smoothly. "We're on the subject of weddings, namely yours and mine. In three days. Unless the waiting period for a marriage license is less in California?" he inquired hopefully.

"I haven't the faintest idea," Brianna informed him. "The subject never interested me before."

"But it does now," he stated firmly.

"Well, I have had more graceful and conventional proposals," she drawled teasingly.

"And accepted none of them," he pointed out calmly.

"True." She granted the point cheerfully, then continued, "Of course, strictly speaking, I'm not even sure if this counts as a proposal. You haven't actually asked 'Will you marry me?' Why, for all you know, I might well have been assuming that your parents and brothers and sisters were just stopping by on their way to a family reunion at oh, say—Disneyland."

"No, you wouldn't assume that," Cane assured her kindly. "Common sense would have told you that, since my parents live in Florida, Disney World would have been much more convenient for them. Besides, when you get to know my father, you'll realize that he hates crowds and would never willingly set foot inside a popular amusement park. Ergo, why else would he be coming to California, if not for his son's wedding?"

"I am awed by the concise clarity of your logic," Brianna said humbly. "I truly apologize. I see now that I was in error. I *have* been proposed to." She drew in a deep breath. "Ahem. Sir, I am deeply aware of the honor you do me. I hereby happily accept your graceful and gracious proposal of marriage and I hope you will forgive my natural maidenly confusion concerning your intentions."

She yelped with surprise as Cane suddenly twisted lithely and rolled her over onto her back. He propped himself up above her on his elbows and growled softly, "You knew from the first moment our eyes met exactly what my intentions were, my lovely lady. You knew all along that I intended to do this to you"—he kissed her deeply— "and this . . ." He bent his head to taste her breast slowly, suckling gently at the tender nipple. "You knew. Confess it . . ." he demanded with mock ferocity, but had his been a serious attempt to project a sense of menace, it would have failed lamentably. The passionate adoration burning in his eyes was unmistakable and revealing. Cane was obviously prepared to pluck rainbows from the sky and spread them in a radiant carpet at her feet if it would please her.

But now Brianna knew what would please her. Her hands reached out to him, pulling his mouth back down to her breast, a wordless, explicit invitation, encouraging him to "compel" her to confess her complicity in their explosive but mutual seduction. She made it clear that she was ready to "confess," and just as ready to thoroughly incriminate herself all over again!

The sheet on the bed might have been pure white, but Cane shattered the spectrum into a rainbow of sensation, coloring Brianna with the bright reds and oranges of passion. His tongue was a red lick of flame, scorching streaks of hot desire wherever it flickered across her body, dyeing her skin with the dusky flush of urgency. He had resolutely controlled the cautious pace of their first union, moving with deliberation and careful patience to ease the sharp shock of first possession, but now the need for slow consummation was gone. There was no barrier between them.

Brianna moved restlessly beneath Cane, ready, wanting, her hands reaching out blindly to enclose, caress and guide him, urging him to confirm his possession. "Ahhh . . . Please, Cane . . . I need . . . I want . . ." Her soft, incoherent pleas were enormously exciting and Cane groaned thickly, shuddering with a spasm of intense pleasure as she again welcomed him into the secret center of all mystery and delight. Instinctively she voluptuously established the fluid rhythm of the rotation of her hips and his hands slid beneath her buttocks, lifting and holding her against the surging power of his smooth penetration, exquisitely enhancing the sweet receptivity of her generous response.

"Fly, little wild bird. Fly!" he encouraged hoarsely as they balanced, delicately poised, on the threshold of release. She answered him with a jubilant, wordless cry and as he felt her body convulse beneath him with irresistible, ecstatic abandonment, he was free to follow her out into the wide, wild realm of shared rapture.

Seven

If emotions could be compared to colors, hers would have traveled the spectrum all the way from passion's urgent red down to satisfaction's languorous blue, Brianna reflected with sleepy whimsicality.

"Brianna, don't you dare roll over and go to sleep," Cane's voice commanded laughingly from somewhere above her head. He twitched the sheet he had pulled up over them after Brianna had begun to produce a rash of goosebumps from the chill of the air conditioning.

"Mphgm."

"Brianna . . ." There was a distinctly warning note in the repetition of her name.

Brianna opened her eyes slowly and sighed heavily. "are you going to be one of those men who wants to *talk?*" she teased in accents of exaggerated dismay. "I thought men were supposed to be only too happy to roll over and go to sleep . . . er . . . afterwards. Besides, what else is there to talk about?" She pitched her voice in smug tones of affected reassurance. "I've already promised to do the honorable thing by you. I'll marry you, even if you're not pregnant, my dear."

There was a long, appalled silence. Brianna closed her eyes again and made little snuggling movements, burrowing beneath the sheet to hide her wicked grin.

"Oh my God!" Cane breathed in stunned accents. "I didn't even think . . . I hadn't planned tonight . . . I mean . . ." he floundered helplessly.

Brianna's shoulders were shaking beneath the sheet. "Brianna darling, I'm sorry! Please don't cry. It'll be all right." He tried to lift her and cradle her against him while he attempted to explain. "I wasn't expecting it . . . I mean, I *was*, but just not tonight. I . . ."

He broke off. By now Brianna's whole body was shaking with the force of her emotion, but the muffled whoops of laughter made it obvious to Cane that the threat of an unplanned pregnancy, if it existed at all, was not a contingency that particularly worried his deplorable fiancée. She might have tears in her eyes, but they weren't streaming down her cheeks from some overflowing wellspring of sorrow.

"Brianna Elizabeth Graeme, soon-to-be Taylor—if you live that long!—what the *hell* are you laughing at?" Cane gritted through clenched teeth.

"Ohhh," she groaned, holding her sides. "I'm sorry, I'm sorry, darling," she gasped apologetically. "I just couldn't resist it." She snorted inelegantly as she struggled to choke back her chortles. "It's just that even if you didn't expect 'it' tonight, I'm afraid I did. I went in to see my family doctor first thing this morning and he started me on the pill. I know it takes a while for it to take effect, but we should still be safe because I'm pretty regular and this is the safe time of my cycle, according to Doctor Joe."

She peeped up at him. He glowered down at her. She smiled tentatively, but the unrepentant twinkle in her eyes spoiled the picture of contrition she was trying to paint.

"You are a devil unconfined," Cane said softly.

"I know," she sighed in sad agreement. She allowed her head to droop despondently and embellished her chosen role with a daintily pathetic sniff.

He patted his naked side searchingly. "Sorry. I seem to have left my handkerchief in my other suit." The words were curt but the tone was filled with rueful amusement.

That was one of the things she liked about Cane, Brianna thought contentedly. He could take a joke. Of course, he could probably hand one out too, she reminded herself.

"Um, Cane? I'm awake now," she informed him sedately. "Did you want to talk to me about something?"

"I don't know. Have you got any more bombshells tucked up your sleeves?" he asked suspiciously.

"Of course not," she denied indignantly. She sat up and waved her bare arms in demonstration. "Look, Ma, no sleeves." The sheet promptly fell down to her waist.

"If your Ma saw you right now, your Pa would probably shoot first and ask me questions later," Cane observed dryly as he punched up a pillow and leaned back against the headboard of the bed. "Of course, *I* have no objections to the view," he continued, leering appreciatively. He patted the pillow beside him invitingly and said, "Come make yourself comfortable."

She scooted backward obediently and, after arranging her own pillow to her satisfaction, settled comfortably beside him, linking hands with him and leaning contentedly against the warm support of his arm. "Well?"

"Well, since the subject did happen to come up" —he paused pregnantly—"what about children?"

"I like children," she answered promptly.

"That's abstract. Would you like *our* children?" he asked specifically.

"Yes," she said decisively. "I would. In a couple of years. I'm not quite ready yet but"—she shot him a sensually scorching look—"we could practice a lot in the meantime, couldn't we?"

"Practice makes perfect," Cane agreed in a strangled voice. If he'd had a collar on, he would have been loosening it to ease the sudden constriction around his throat.

"Anything else?" Brianna asked blandly.

"Yes. Are you in the mood for a cold shower?" Cane queried grimly.

"What a horrible idea!" She rejected his suggestion vehemently.

"Okay, a warm shower then. It's about time for me to take you home. Do you think your parents will still be awake? The sooner we tell them we're getting married, the better. I don't suppose your mother is going to appreciate having to plan even a very small wedding in such a short time." He didn't stop to think that her parents might justifiably object to the mere *fact* of a wedding in such a short time—he and Brianna had known each other for less than forty-eight hours—but the thought wouldn't have bothered him anyway. They were made for each other and time had nothing to do with it. Brianna would explain to her parents.

"I have a better idea," she countered. "Let's do take a warm shower, but let's not take me home." She patted the mattress. "I'm sure this bed is big enough for both of us."

"No."

"No shower?" She was purposely dense.

"Yes shower. No, you can't stay all night, not for three more days." Cane was magnificently patient.

"Why not? Look at it this way," she argued earnestly. "If I move in with you now, before the wedding, there'd be just that much more room for your relatives out at the ranch. We could probably fit the whole family in. Think of the motel bills we'd save."

"I can afford it," Cane declared firmly.

"Don't you want a thrifty wife?" Brianna teased.

"Thrift," he announced austerely, "is an admirable trait. It is not, however, the one which I consider most essential in a wife."

"Oh?" Brianna gulped the bait, hook, line and sinker. "What trait *do* you consider essential in a wife?" she asked with considerable interest.

"It's actually a collection of qualities," Cane pronounced gravely, "and you might want to lump them all together under one general heading as sort of an all-purpose survival trait. One of its primary components might best be described as: Knowing when to quit."

Brianna laughed. "You do know how to make a point," she said admiringly.

"Lady, I know how to make a lot of things," Cane declared, "including"—he swung his long legs over the edge of the bed and stood up—"soapsuds in the shower." He held out his hand. "C'mon. I'll give you a firsthand demonstration. It's called 'Cleanliness is next to . . . uh . . .'"

"Lust?" she suggested helpfully while he pulled her to her feet.

"Yeah!" he agreed enthusiastically. "Let's go lather up some good clean lust."

It was a good thing that California wasn't currently in the midst of a drought, Brianna reflected cheerfully while Cane—finally—drove the truck toward the ranch. Their shared shower had been both prolonged and thorough. Why hadn't she realized before what an erotic and exciting texture there was to soap-slick skin? And it was handy—she winced slightly at the small mental pun—to have someone to scrub your back. Her spine had been scoured from nape to coccyx, including that precise, irritating spot in the middle of your back that you can't quite reach, no matter what contortions you employ.

"Do you think your parents are still awake?"

Cane's quiet question interrupted her very pleasant reverie. She temporarily tucked away the tactile memory of the feel of his strongly muscled back rippling beneath the massage of her fingers while she spread the rich lather across his wide shoulders. "I doubt it. Usually they go to bed pretty early and they gave up waiting for me to come home from a date a long time ago." She yawned widely. "Besides, I've come up with a really effective way for us to announce our imminent nuptials. Since you won't let me stay at your apartment"—

her disapproving sniff was eloquently expressive—
"how about if you sleep out at the ranch tonight?
I'll share my bed with you," she offered generously.
"Then Mom can catch us *flagrante delicto* tomorrow morning. We won't have to announce a thing!"

"Effective is not precisely the word I would choose
to describe that scheme," Cane retorted crisply.

"You don't like it, huh? Well, how about . . . ?"

"How about if we simply say 'We're getting married in three days, Mom and Dad,' and see how
that works?" Cane interrupted firmly.

"But Cane . . ."

"No, Brianna."

"Spoilsport."

"You betcha."

"Okay." She sighed regretfully and capitulated.
"We'll tell them tomorrow morning. You can come
out to the ranch early and have breakfast with us
and we'll announce it then. If we dump some
champagne in the orange juice we can still add a
little pizazz to this announcement, I suppose."

"Don't worry," he consoled her. "I'll make sure
that you get plenty of 'pizazz' after we're married."

Brianna laughed softly, deep in the back of her
throat. "Yeahhh," she breathed in reminiscent
agreement. Cane would supply *everything* she
needed.

The house was dark, except for the small hall
light that was always left on until the last one out
was safely home again. Brianna flicked the light
off and made her way cautiously down the hall to
her bedroom. She closed the door quietly behind
her but didn't immediately reach out to the light
switch. Instead she moved surefootedly toward
the pale outline of the window, automatically skirt-

ing the familiar furniture, until she reached the cushioned window seat. She curled up comfortably and rested her forearms on the sill, looking out soberly over the starlit view.

She had left this peaceful scene mere hours ago, a girl in spirit, if not one by strict chronological reckoning. She had returned a woman, profoundly committed to a man she had known two days. The view from her window was the same, but the landscape of her life had changed cataclysmically. Her family would welcome Cane enthusiastically, for himself, and as a stabilizing influence, Brianna thought wryly—that is, they would once they got over the immediate shock of the hasty marriage! But from Brianna's point of view, Cane had swept into her life with the irresistible impact of an earthquake, until *terra* wasn't *firma* anymore.

Of course, there were compensations. Her smile was sleek with secret knowledge and she stretched slowly with the smooth languor of fulfilled sensuality. The old days, the independent, free-ranging ways, were irrevocably gone. She flew in tandem now, but Cane had shown her a new realm, a new territory to explore, one which, however, she could enter only at his side or in his arms.

She shook her head and shrugged with pensive acceptance as she rose from her seat—no one could have everything in life. Cane was worth a great deal of compromise. Her smile sharpened with a twist of mockery. Talk about making a virtue of necessity! She really had no choice. She and Cane were the halves of a whole. If she left him and lost him, it would maim her. It was a special sweet terror to know that another held the wholeness of her soul in his hands.

But she wasn't one to waste worry on what she couldn't change. Her sleep that short night was deep and restful, as befitted a crystal-clear conscience and a satisfied . . . mind. She woke with a smile on her face. Even the shrill sound of her travel alarm had lost its usual power to spoil her mood—she had been known to throw the unwelcome summoner across the room upon occasion! Brianna was a naturally slow starter on most mornings.

Her mother eyed her askance when she bounded into the kitchen and chirruped a cheery "Good morning, Mom. Cook some extra sausages and eggs, please. I could eat Beelzebub, with or without his saddle and shoes. I'll set the table for you," and started rattling plates and flatware in an uncharacteristically enthusiastic manner.

It was not that Brianna was ever grudging or uncooperative about doing her fair share of the chores whenever she was home—she always worked with a will. But Mary had rarely known her volatile daughter to perform her share of the early morning chores with more than polite silence, at least until after the first cup of coffee had given her reluctant circulatory system a stiff jolt of caffeine. Such early-hour good humor was highly suspect and Mary suspected that she knew exactly what could account for it.

"Had a nice time last night, did you?" she called after Brianna's retreating back as it disappeared into the dining room.

"Loverly!" The ready reply floated back in warbling accents. "Nice" simply didn't do justice to the time she had had, Brianna thought smugly while she shuffled the plates out in the appropriate place settings. And one for Cane . . .

The family was assembling for breakfast and as Mary and Brianna came through to the dining room bearing the covered platters of scrambled eggs, sausage and buttermilk biscuits, Drew joked, "I think Bree was definitely gone too long on this last project. She forgot how many there are in the family and set out one too many places."

"Not in the least, little brother," Brianna retorted coolly. "I can still count. Your mistake is simply that you didn't know that we're about to add another member to the family." As though they had rehearsed it, Cane's knock sounded on the front door precisely a split second after she had finished speaking. "Excuse me, please," she said sweetly, "I'll go let Cane in," and made a faultless exit, leaving dropped jaws and stunned incredulity behind her.

She opened the door for Cane and announced blithely, with a beaming smile, "Good morning, darling. I have just given the family a hint about us." There was a beguiling smile of mischief apparent in the twinkle in her eye.

Cane's smile immediately slipped into an expression of questioning concern. He had already developed a well-founded mistrust of that particular expression of artful innocence. "Brianna . . ." he began sternly.

"It was a very *gentle* hint, sweetheart," she assured him instantly and stood on tiptoe to fling her arms around his neck. The kiss she gave him was guaranteed to distract him while it inspired every corpuscle in his body to perform morning calisthenics with verve and zeal. With a low, hungry groan, Cane used his free hand to pull her hard against his body. The other hand held a brown paper sack that clinked.

"Mmmm. What a wonderful way to start the day," Brianna murmured with immense satisfaction. "Heaps better than hot homemade waffles and real maple syrup." She plastered herself against Cane, nuzzling his neck and giving an inspired imitation of a somewhat overenthusiastic boa constrictor. Her highly reprehensible sense of humor was running amok.

"Brianna, for God's sake!" he choked on a strangled gasp. "I have to go in there and face your parents, especially your father. Cut it out!"

"Oh pooh," she scoffed. "Where's your sense of adventure?"

"Right in line behind my sense of propriety," he retorted crisply. "I want to make a reasonably good impression on your family, not give them a graphic demonstration of one of the reasons we're going to get married in such a hurry!"

"Oh! Well, when you put it that way . . ." She released him with manifest reluctance. "What's in the sack?" she asked, with the direct curiosity of a child.

"Your 'pizazz,'" he informed her with a grin. "I stopped by an all-night liquor store on the way home last night and picked up a couple of bottles of champagne. They've been chilling in my refrigerator. You did make up some orange juice for breakfast, didn't you?"

She laughed delightedly. "There's a whole pitcher of it. What delicious decadence, champagne for breakfast! Someone ought to write a song about it: 'My baby gives me cold champagne in the morning and hot, hot love in the night.'" She hummed a throaty bar of impromptu music. "What d'you think? Will it make the top twenty?" she solicited his opinion.

"I think we'd better go in and see how your parents are reacting to your *gentle* hint," Cane decided firmly.

"Rats!" she declared mildly. "I was hoping you wouldn't notice that I was stalling."

"Honey, I notice everything about you," he told her dryly, "*especially* when you're stalling. Let's go. I'll protect you."

"That's easy for you to say," she muttered as they walked down the hall together. She grabbed his hand for moral support and he squeezed it encouragingly. No wonder he was so calm, she thought with some asperity. *He* got to tell *his* parents about their forthcoming marriage over the telephone. *She* had to brazen it out face to face with *her* parents.

Just before they reached the dining room door, Cane pulled her to a halt and whispered practically, "Let's stash this champagne somewhere until after all the fur has flown and the dust has settled."

"An excellent idea," Brianna agreed promptly. "You go on ahead while I find a good place to put it." She reached for the paper bag.

Cane held the sack back out of her reach. "Hey, what happened to 'for better or for worse'? And," he asked pointedly, "exactly how gentle was that hint you dropped?"

"Does 'for better et cetera' start even *before* we get married?" she asked cautiously.

"Yes!" he said definitely.

"I *knew* you were going to say that!" she said

mournfully. She squared her shoulders and suggested, "Why don't you leave the champagne on the couch. That way we can grab it easily if we have to make a hasty exit."

"I don't think you should be so reassuring," Cane said wryly. "I wouldn't want to suffer from overconfidence." He laid the bottles of champagne gently on their sides and then slipped his arm around Brianna's shoulders. "Let's get it over with. I only wish I didn't suddenly feel like a draftee in the Light Brigade right before they made their final charge."

"I told you we should have let Mom catch us in bed together," Brianna reminded him. "See all the trouble it would have saved?"

"People who say 'I told you so' are only slightly less aggravating than people who say 'I'm just doing this for your own good,'" Cane warned her.

"Yes, Cane," she agreed meekly.

He didn't make the mistake of believing that she would remain subdued for long. He urged her toward the dining room and together they stepped into the room to face her family. It was interesting, and probably profoundly psychologically significant, that Brianna looked first to her mother while Cane met Adam's eye firmly and directly.

Brianna drew in a deep breath and announced baldly, "Mom and Dad, Cane and I are getting married in three days."

There was a thundering silence.

Adam looked over at his wife and his silent message was easily translated by everyone present as "*How do we handle* THIS?"

Adam's confidence in his wife was quickly justified. She smiled warmly at Cane and said,

"Welcome to the family, Cane. I can't say that Brianna's announcement is wholly unexpected, but I do admit to being surprised by the speed of the decision." Her voice became brisk. "Don't just stand there in the doorway, children. Come in and sit down. Breakfast is getting cold and I think we could all do with a little respite to digest and then discuss your plans. Alex, pass the eggs to your sister. Andrew, start the sausages around, please."

Brianna smiled proudly. She had known she could count on her family. She and Cane took their seats.

Cane regarded Mary with undisguised astonishment. Whatever reaction he had envisioned, it had not included such open friendliness and unmistakable sang-froid when presented with a stranger (practically) as her imminent prospective son-in-law. He sat for a moment, balancing the platter of eggs that Brianna had just passed to him, staring blankly down at the yellow curds as though they were some wildly exotic type of food he had never before encountered. Brianna's soft "Cane?" roused him from his reverie. He served himself and passed the platter on, but his mind was obviously not on breakfast. Being Cane, he went directly to the point. "Uh . . . Mary, do you mind my asking *why* you aren't surprised that Brianna and I are going to get married?"

"Of course not, Cane. It's very simple." Mary's tone was soft and coolly amused. "You just haven't known Brianna long enough to realize how *totally* uncharacteristic her reaction to you was. We've" —her graceful gesture encompassed the other members of the family—"never seen her respond to anyone, to any man," she amended specifically, "the way she did to you. Please don't take this amiss, but if you weren't so thoroughly human and . . . and *practical*, I might suspect you of being some sort of warlock who's worked a wondrous enchantment on her. No other man—and you may believe me that the previous competition was both extensive and determined—ever made the slightest impact on her dedicated independence. And by the way, I do hope you're not the jealous type because Brianna has a large number of men friends, most of whom were once hopeful boyfriends who finally settled for what they could get, which was friendship. You won't be particularly popular with them for a while, but they'll eventually accept the inevitable, just as we have. As I said, once we saw Brianna's reaction, we knew it was just a matter of time, but I must admit that we didn't expect it to be such a *short* time."

Brianna ground her teeth audibly. "M-o-ther!"

"Well, dear, he did ask," Mary said imperturbably.

Brianna concentrated on thoroughly dissecting an innocent sausage.

Cane's voice was thoughtful. "So it wasn't my reaction to Brianna that . . . er . . . tipped you off."

Mary was apologetic. "Well, we could tell that you weren't *indifferent* to Brianna, Cane dear, but of course we didn't know you well enough to judge your reactions all that accurately. And besides . . ." she hesitated tactfully.

Cane's slow smile had definite mischievous overtones. "And besides, most men react that way to Brianna," he finished smoothly.

"*Do* . . . you . . . people . . . mind!" Brianna demanded. "You could at least have the courtesy to gossip about me *behind* my back!" Her face felt like it had a third-degree sunburn.

Mercifully they concentrated on their meal for a while. Brianna decided privately that her mother was going to get ragweed instead of roses for her next birthday and as for Cane, she was sure that a suitable revenge would eventually occur to her. She shot a glance at her father from beneath the screen of her lowered lids and thick eyelashes. He was observing Cane with a thoughtful and purposeful gleam in his eyes. She grinned secretly to herself. Her mother might have set the official tone of the family's reaction, but Cane needn't think that he was going to get off without an interview with her father. Alex and Drew would undoubtedly put their four cents worth in too at the earliest opportunity. A loving family was a wonderful thing to have, but it did have certain drawbacks. Everyone felt entitled to express an opinion.

Come to think of it, *she* had at times expressed, with considerable sisterly candor, opinions concerning certain of Alex's previous girlfriends. All things considered, she decided sensibly, it was better not to interfere with an established family tradition. After all, she might not approve of Alex's next girlfriend and she certainly intended to reserve the right to tell him so! Besides, Alex liked Cane and it was more likely that, in the excess of masculine fellow-feeling, he would tell Cane about *her* faults, bad habits and ticklish feet!

Obedient to Mary's guidance, conversation at the breakfast table avoided the subject uppermost on all minds, but as soon as everyone had reached the "last bite of biscuit and jelly" stage, Brianna said rather wistfully, "Cane, could I have my 'pizazz' now?"

Cane laughed, rose from his chair and dropped a kiss on the top of her head. "Sure, sweetheart. You get the glasses, I'll retrieve the 'pizazz.'" He excused himself and left the dining room.

"'Pizazz'?" Alex asked the question for the rest of the family.

"Champagne," Brianna explained. "Cane brought a couple of bottles so we could toast our engagement. The rest is a private joke. Mom, can we use the Waterford champagne glasses?"

"Of course," Mary agreed promptly, "just as long as you don't intend to fling them at the fireplae after the toast. Let's clear away the breakfast remains first and rinse off the crystal. Cane"—he had reentered the room carrying the two bottles of Mumm's—"bring the champagne into the kitchen and we'll put it into the refrigerator to stay chilled while we clean up and get the glasses ready."

They assembled again in the family room and in proper form toasted the impending nuptials and the principal participants. Then Mary brought up the subject of just how "impending" the wedding actually was.

"You weren't really serious when you said 'three days,' were you, Brianna?"

"Well . . . not exactly," Brianna admitted. Cane stiffened beside her. *He* had been serious! "The thing is," she continued before he could speak, "neither of us knew exactly how long it takes to get a license, but we figured that it couldn't take more than three days, so that seemed a reasonable time, and there'll be blood tests too, I guess.

Dr. Joe can do those for both of us. I was going to call the county office this morning to find out exactly what we have to do."

"Reasonable time . . ." her mother said faintly. "Brianna Elizabeth Graeme, three days is *not* a reasonable time in which to plan and hold a wedding. Cane's family, the flowers, the church, your dress, Aunt Agatha . . ."

"No! Absolutely not! I draw the line at Aunt Agatha," Brianna said heatedly. "And it is a reasonable time if all we want is a small, quiet church ceremony with only the *closest* family present. I don't want ten bridesmaids, a dress with a long train and a coach and four white horses to take me to the church," she exaggerated with a smile. "We can have a reception later . . ." She paused as inspiration obviously struck her. "Well, in fact, the barbecue is already on the calendar and you did tell me to invite *everyone*. . . ." Her voice trailed away and she stared at her mother with the gravest suspicion dawning in her expressive eyes.

"Mother!" she said in shocked accents. "You didn't plan the barbecue with this in mind, did you?" Mary Graeme had a well-deserved reputation within the family for foresight, but that would be going too far!

Her mother had the grace to look slightly embarrassed. "Well, I certainly didn't plan it as a *wedding* reception," she denied mildly, "but I told you we weren't surprised about your deciding to get married. I thought the barbecue might do very well as an engagement party. You haven't ever been noted for your patience, Brianna darling," Mary pointed out fairly, "and your father and I always knew that when you fell in love, you wouldn't be very patient about that either."

Cane smothered a laugh and Brianna blushed. They alone knew very well just how *im*patient she had been when she fell in love.

Eight

Her mother had known exactly what she was talking about, Brianna realized ruefully. They *couldn't* plan and hold a wedding in just three days!

The license proved to be the first impediment. Even with Dr. Joe's enthusiastic cooperation—and congratulations—it would take at least two days to get the required blood tests processed and reported, including the mandatory rubella test for Brianna because she was—Cane shot her a balefully reproving look when she chuckled reminiscently—of childbearing age. Since he was a new patient, Dr. Joe subjected Cane to a brief but comprehensive physical before certifying that he was sound of wind and limb, although he jokingly questioned Cane's soundness of mind for wanting to take on such a handful as Brianna. While Brianna glared impartially at both men, Cane agreed that perhaps Dr. Joe should examine his head while he was at it and, for good measure, asked for a prescription for superstrength vitamins. Brianna was heard to mutter that maybe she ought to get her head examined too, but the doctor silenced her feeble comeback by announcing that since he had been caring for that same head from the day he had brought it into the light, he had no need to examine it further. It was his considered professional diagnosis that she had somehow finally knocked some sense into that hard noggin of hers and Cane was just what the doctor had ordered for her. Brianna sweetly commended her old friend on his accomplished bedpan manner and promised to save him a special portion of the barbecued pig at the party in two weeks. Cane hustled her out of the office before she could say which part!

"I got the distinct impression that your Dr. Joe might tend to turn a trifle touchy whenever he has to patch up his original job on you," Cane commented drily as he herded her toward the truck in the parking lot of the medical center.

"'Quarrelsomely crabby' is more like it," Brianna corrected exasperatedly. "I'm the only one he ever gives the tetanus shots to. Dee, his office nurse, gives them to everyone else, but Dr. Joe likes to punctuate his lectures to me with jabs from the needle. Last year I accidently gashed my hand on some barbed wire and, in addition to the tetanus booster shot, I had a fifteen-minute lecture from him about wearing gloves while working wire. It was only two lousy little stitches, for crying out loud"— she pointed to the minuscule scar on the fleshy part of her palm near the base of her thumb— "but you would have thought he'd had to do major reconstructive surgery. And it wasn't my fault anyway. I didn't have my gloves with me and Alex just asked me to hold a strand for a minute while he got a wire cutter. I didn't have a good grip on it when Alex let it go and it swung around and bit me. Could have happened to anybody," she grumbled.

Cane didn't try to resist the obvious. "But you're not 'anybody,'" he pointed out significantly, "and I rather imagine that Dr. Joe was always afraid that there might come a day when he wouldn't be able to patch up his original job anymore."

Brianna changed the subject. She had no intention of treading on the thin ice of *that* particular topic! As he swung the truck out of the parking lot she directed, "Since we've done all we can do for the moment about the legalities, you can drop me off at the church. Take a right at the next corner." She added smoothly, "I know you need to get back out to the site and anyway, Mom's going to pick me up there after I've talked to the minister. She's down at the Flower Fair now, arranging for the flowers to decorate the church, and she's left a cold lunch ready for you men because we're going shopping for a wedding dress this afternoon."

It was a successful distraction. "Are you going to pick out a sexy, sheer nightgown for our wedding night?" Cane's eyes gleamed with hopeful anticipation.

"I doubt if I'd ever get my money's worth of wear out of it if I did," Brianna observed lightly as Cane pulled up in front of the church.

"I can pretty well guarantee that you won't," he admitted with cheerful candor and then continued with unmistakable relish, "but just think of the fun I'll have taking it off you. It'll be like

Christmas and my birthday all wrapped up in one gorgeous present!"

A smile of gleeful mischief lifted the corners of her mouth. "Does that mean that you don't plan to . . . ah . . . *unwrap* your present at all before our wedding night?" Her voice was a husky, teasing purr.

Cane's answer was a slow smile, full of masculine promise. "Brianna darling," he drawled softly, "if I tell you that as a little boy I could never stand to wait until Christmas Day to open my presents, and if I tell you that I haven't changed one bit now that I'm all grown up, will that answer your question?"

"*Completely*," she said with satisfaction.

Brianna and her mother finished off a hard afternoon of successful shopping with the purchase of three large Sam's Special Pizzas, extra sauce, extra cheese, one with anchovies, two without, and two family salads, hold the dressing. Cold beer and hot pizza were always a hit with hungry ranchers.

While Brianna braced the three boxes of pizza and the two salad containers between her feet, Mary maneuvered deftly through thick traffic until she reached the road leading out of town, back toward the ranch. "Remember what Dad said the last time you got a speeding ticket?" Brianna teased as her mother accelerated smoothly.

Mary grimaced. "Vividly. But they never patrol the back stretches of road during the rush hour. Besides, we don't want the pizza to get soggy. Your father hates soggy pizza."

"So it would be *his* fault if you got a speeding ticket," Brianna deduced with considerable amusement.

"Naturally," Mary agreed blandly. "A pertinent lesson of wifehood, dear daughter. When caught in an embarrassing situation, always remember that if you can make him believe that it's *his* fault, he can't yell at *you*." Mother and daughter laughed companionably at the family joke. Adam Graeme might grumble and growl, but he never yelled at his womenfolk.

Brianna wondered how Cane would react when the inevitable disagreements arose? Would he roar or rumble? Was he a slow burn or a hot flash fire? She was realistic enough to know that, no matter how much they loved each other, there would still be times when their temperaments and opinions would collide. They would fight, but then they could make up. How they could make up!

"That smile is positively indecent, Brianna," Mary remarked observantly. "And speaking of Cane, did he ever manage to contact his parents?"

Brianna adjusted her telltale expression to approximate innocence. "Not before we left this morning. He was going to try again this afternoon and if there was still no answer at their condominium, he was going to call his older sister. She usually knows where to reach them if they've gone out of town, and besides, Cane wants to invite all of his brothers and sisters to our wedding."

"I hope they'll all be able to come. Cane's parents will have the guest room, of course, and we'll fit in as many others as we can. Alex and Drew can sleep in the trailer," Mary said, plotting bed space aloud.

"I offered to move in with Cane before the wed-

ding so that one of his family could have my bed,"
Brianna announced, "but he wouldn't let me."

"How depressingly proper of him," Mary com-
miserated, tongue in cheek. "You'll have to cure
him of that."

"I'll make it my first . . . well, maybe my second
. . . priority as a wife," Brianna promised.

"A wife." Her mother sighed. "How strange that
sounds. It seems like only yesterday . . . Well, never
mind that," she said briskly. "At least we don't
have to have a mother/daughter talk."

"No. If I remember correctly, we did that when I
was about seven years old," Brianna said with a
chuckle.

"Good. But Brianna"—her mother's voice lost
its light, teasing tone—"you have thought about
what marriage to Cane means, haven't you? I'm
not questioning your love for each other," she
added hastily, before Brianna could speak. "Anyone
with one eye open can see that you two are in
love, but marriage is more than that. It's living
together, blending the two different lifestyles into
a shared one. Do you love Cane enough to do
that? Does he mean more to you than your freedom to rove?

"Don't answer *me*," Mary finished gravely, lifting a hand from the steering wheel in a gesture of
negation. "You owe those answers to yourself and
to Cane. You're leaping into marriage, my dear. I
want both of you to have a happy landing."

Brianna was thoughtful and silent for a long
moment before she said quietly, "I have thought
about it, Mom. I started thinking about it on
Monday, that very first day, because I knew already that I was going to marry Cane as soon as

he asked me." Her smile was a little sad, a little wistful. "I knew from the moment I saw him that the old, free-roving life was over for me."

She stared out through the car's windshield at the dry, rolling hillsides and continued soberly, "I'm not going to say that I won't miss it. I will. I'll miss it very much and I can't pretend otherwise." She sighed. "I know that you and Dad have never really understood *why* I had to wander, although you let me go so freely that it was always easy to come home again. Even now I don't think that I can really explain the 'why' to you. Somehow any words I can come up with seem inadequate, imprecise."

Her voice was soft, meditative. "Uncle Ben was the only one who ever understood, you know, but that was because he had the same compulsion to . . . to . . . track the wind." She seemed to search for words. "It's as though you can hear a song in the wind when it blows past you and you have to follow it to hear the rest of the melody." She gestured almost helplessly. "Oh, it's impossible! Words just can't explain, but it doesn't matter any more. I know that I can't have Cane and my old life too. The wind doesn't sing to him." Her words were filled with calm acceptance when she finished simply, "Life is choices. I choose Cane."

Both women were silent until Mary turned the car onto the rough ranch track. Then Brianna declared suddenly, with the sound of a grin in her voice, "There will, however, be compensations."

Mary was a woman, as well as a mother, and she had observed the ardent hunger in Cane's gaze whenever it touched Brianna. "I imagine that there will be," she agreed demurely, with a soft laugh of her own.

When they reached the ranch, Brianna discovered that it really didn't matter that the legalities were going to take longer than originally planned. Again failing to contact his parents at their condominium, Cane had called his older sister, Susan, only to discover that his parents were away on a fishing trip and weren't scheduled to return for two more days. Of course, they would be only too happy to cut short their trip and come back sooner, if they could be contacted, but in a moment of uncharacteristic madness Cane's mother had let his father talk her into "roughing it" at a remote fishing camp well back in the Everglades, where there was no phone.

"Susan said that there was an emergency contact link available through the Rangers and she'd be glad to try to reach Mom and Dad that way," Cane reported glumly as he lounged against a counter in the kitchen, watching Brianna carefully pour a beer into a frosted mug. "Since we can't even get the license until Friday, after the blood test results come back, I told her not to bother. We might as well wait and get married next Monday. That'll give the folks the weekend to get here." He scowled ferociously. "Damn! I hate long engagements!"

"Oh, I do too," Brianna agreed gravely. "A week is my absolute limit for engagements. After that I just live in sin."

Cane growled, shoved himself away from the counter and moved lithely to stand directly in front of her. He reached out and pulled her against his body, cupping her buttocks with his hands to press her lower torso firmly against his hips. He bent his head and nuzzled hungrily at her neck, running little nipping kisses along the side of her throat, up over the angle of her jaw, pausing to time the throb of her pulse beneath the soft thin skin at her temple with a long slow kiss before retracing his path downward. Brianna, who was severely hampered by the brimming mug of beer she still held in one hand and the empty can she clutched in the other, participated as enthusiastically as those dual handicaps allowed. The liquid splash of good malt beer splattering on her mother's clean kitchen floor and dampening her bare ankles was a clear indication that Cane's kisses had affected her concentration as well as her pulse rate.

"I hope that you weren't really very thirsty," she murmured as she arched her neck obediently in response to his nudge.

"Why?" he muttered in a muffled voice while his lips began a leisurely exploration of the vulnerable underside of her chin.

"Because I think I just poured half of your beer out on the floor."

"Can't you do two things at once?" he laughed softly.

"Not when one of them is concentrating on being kissed by you!" she admitted easily. "I have *my* priorities straight!"

Cane's family obviously had its priorities straight too. They all, babes in arms included, would be arriving Saturday and Sunday from various points of the compass to attend the wedding, as would Cane's other partner, Scott, and his wife, Cane's cousin Cindy. Brianna's family would be more sparsely represented. Only one uncle, her father's younger brother, plus his wife and son could come in time and her mother's formidable Aunt Agatha was—fortunately—away on an extended cruise. So the wedding party would be decidedly unbalanced, numerically speaking, but as Mary pointed out with inescapable logic, if they started to invite even the closest of friends to equalize the numbers somewhat, they would soon find it impossible to draw a line without mortally offending those who considered themselves equally close friends. Much safer to strictly limit attendance to family.

"See, Alex, I told you that you should have gotten married a long time ago and had a bunch of kids," Brianna teased, waving a piece of breakfast toast at him for emphasis as they all sat around the table on Friday morning. "That would have helped to balance the numbers a little."

Alex merely grunted. He was still working on his first cup of coffee.

Cane sat silently beside her, looking a trifle heavy-eyed. He had "unwrapped" his present several times on each of the preceding nights and, because he steadfastly refused either to allow Brianna to spend the night at his apartment or to let her drive home by herself, he was missing out on considerably more sleep than his beloved was. She dozed comfortably on his shoulder while he drove her home and then slept like a rock from the moment her head hit the pillow on her chaste bed at the ranch. Cane, on the other hand, still had a twenty-five minute drive back to his apartment before he could attain the lonely comfort of his rumpled bed, not to mention a twenty-five minute earlier start to his day, just so he could breakfast with Brianna and the family. It was a very good thing that he was blessed with a naturally resilient constitution *and* that they were getting married in three days!

"Anyway," Brianna pointed out blithely, "we're all going to be 'family' as soon as Cane and I exchange the rings. . . . Good grief, Cane!" she yelped in dismay. "We forgot all about getting the wedding rings."

"No, we didn't forget," Cane said calmly. "We have an appointment at the jewelry store this morning, right after we stop by Dr. Joe's office to pick up the blood test results and the certificates to take with us to the license bureau. The jeweler will engrave the rings we choose and have them ready for me to pick up on Monday morning, before the ceremony. Pass the blackberry jam, please."

In the ensuing days, Brianna made lists and Cane made sure that the things that Brianna forgot to put on her lists still got done, and finally Monday morning dawned, hot and clear.

Brianna stretched lazily as the early morning light spilled warmly over her, streaming through the sparkling windows she had deliberately left uncovered the night before. She had been determined to wake up early without resorting to a jarring summons from her alarm clock, fully intending to savor every possible moment of this day, the day she would become Cane's wife in legal name, as she was his already by choice and physical bond. Tonight she would drift down into sleep within the protective, possessive shelter of his arms. No more for her would there be a reluctant scramble back into clothes when all she really wanted to do was to cuddle next to him, to dream the sweet erotic dreams which he would turn into glorious reality as soon as they wakened together in the morning. She had been patient— well, semi-patient—long enough!

She sat up in bed and listened intently. The house was heavily silent, filled with the peculiarly expectant hush that pervades a home full of soundly sleeping people who will soon awake to begin a day crammed with hectic activity. Those dear people, her family, Cane's family, would stand together today to watch her start the outward transition from wanderer, free-rover, into wife, a transition infinitely more complex and difficult than the one she had already made, that secret transition from girl into woman.

Life was just chock full of surprises, Brianna thought wryly, and her life more than most, but after all, she added fairly, she'd made a career of them. She laughed softly to herself as she slid silently out of bed. She couldn't deny that Cane was the most exciting, as well as the most unexpected, surprise life had ever sent her way! *Thank you, life!*

She slipped into a colorful light cotton caftan and made her way stealthily into the kitchen where she brewed the morning's first pot of coffee. While she was waiting for the coffee to drip, she toyed briefly with the idea of calling Cane to say good morning, but after due consideration—and a sharp glance at the clock—she regretfully discarded the impulse. Poor man. He had been looking a trifle haggard recently—she grinned reminiscently—and he *had* been up late last night. Unfortunately, she thought, for the most impeccably innocent of reasons . . . darn it. Since his family had started arriving, they hadn't had an unchaperoned moment to themselves. There was a saying that you can't miss what you never had, but now Brianna knew *exactly* what she was missing!

She poured herself a mug of steaming coffee, sugared it lightly, and strolled out onto the patio, breathing deeply of the fresh morning air. Cane's apartment was comfortably spacious but suddenly she was visited by the uneasy suspicion that she was going to feel claustrophobic whenever she stepped outside it and found herself continually hemmed by concrete and asphalt. With a sharp shock she realized that she had never actually *lived* in a city, or even a town, before. Oh sure, she had visited them, even stayed for several weeks, but always on her own terms, always on a *temporary* basis. She had been free to move on, free to find the open spaces and relief from the pressure of the teeming throngs of people, all hurrying, scurrying, racing about furiously with no time or thought to slow and listen to the music in the wind. For a brief, wild moment her throat closed with panic, but a vision of Cane's dear, strong face rose in her mind's eye and she relaxed. He would understand. They'd work it out. They *would* work it out, she promised herself fiercely. It would be all right.

There was no slightest shadow of disquiet, nothing but calm confidence and joyful eagerness in Brianna's expression behind the short, sheer veil when she walked serenely down the aisle toward Cane, her hand resting lightly on her father's steady arm. The tempo of the pulse in her tanned throat, revealed by the proud lift of her head and the deep square neckline of her crisp, white, embroidered eyelet cotton dress, was steady and unhurried. The scalloped hem of the full, knee-length skirt flared and swirled rhythmically and gracefully with each measured step and the wide, scalloped flounce that edged the neckline of the fitted bodice rose and fell smoothly with her slow, even breaths. Her eyes saw only Cane.

Cane's eyes had not left her face from the moment she and her father had appeared at the back of the church. Somehow, even before the triumphant peal of the organ could announce the presence of the bride, he had known that she was there. He pivoted to face down the aisle and the fierce blaze of joy on his face produced stinging eyes and large lumps in the throats of every woman present, and most of the men, had they been honest enough to admit it. Adam swallowed heavily as he walked beside Brianna, but she didn't notice.

She heard only Cane.

"I, Cane, take thee, Brianna . . ."

Their voices were clear, their pledges firmly given. It was their public affirmation of the intensely personal, private reality of their oneness. It was a claiming that transcended mere legal ritual. It was a bonding, a blending, elemental and absolute.

The minister said, "You may kiss the bride."

With gentle hands, Cane brushed the veil away from Brianna's face while she tilted her chin to receive the kiss of marriage. His warm mouth met hers in a kiss in which passion was a promise and commitment was a reality.

"I love you," he whispered as the kiss ended.

"I love you, too," she whispered back.

Formally, ceremoniously, he offered his arm for

the walk back down the aisle, as was traditional. But as soon as they were out of earshot of the congregation, their families, he bent his head and muttered, "If we make a run for it right now, we can be back at the apartment, with the door locked, within five minutes and completely naked in six."

"Five and a half if the zipper on the back of my dress cooperates and doesn't get stuck," Brianna promised recklessly. She should have known better.

"Now that's an offer I won't refuse." Cane's deep voice brimmed with satisfaction. He immediately altered his course, heading toward the doors at the back of the church.

"Cane Taylor!" Brianna expostulated with a gasp, laughing as she pulled back on his arm, slowing but not entirely stopping his determined stride.

When she continued to tug against his arm, he halted obediently and looked down at her with an expression of inquiring innocence. "Did we forget something? We've already used up a minute and a half," he warned gravely, "but I think we can make up the time if you start to unzip your dress in the car while I'm driving."

"You're a raving lunatic!" she hissed. "I really ought to let you go through with it, just so I could watch you trying to explain to your mother and my mother exactly why we didn't join the rest of the family celebrating at the post-wedding dinner at the ranch." She primmed her mouth, trying to look suitably scandalized, but a helpless gurgle of mirth defeated her.

"Your mother and my mother are both grown women, Brianna darling," Cane informed her loftily, "and between them total eight children and well over sixty plus years of marriage. I wouldn't have to *explain* a thing to them. I might, however, need to *apologize*," he conceded with scrupulous exactitude.

He shot a glance over his shoulder and sighed regretfully. "Anyway, it's too late now. Here comes the family and there goes our chance to slip out for a little legal love in the afternoon."

"Is 'legal' love more fun than the kind we've been doing?" Brianna asked rashly, adopting an expression of deep curiosity. Then she narrowed her eyes and stared at her brand new husband with an air of stern suspicion. "Cane Taylor, have you been holding out on me just because we weren't married?"

Without the slightest struggle, Cane succumbed to base temptation. "Honey," he drawled dangerously, "I do promise most solemnly that I haven't been holding *anything* out on you. In fact"—his smile was distilled wickedness—"if those pills that the doctor gave you don't work, you might soon have exceedingly tangible proof that you've been getting everything . . ."

"Cane!" she interrupted hastily. The hot scarlet of her blush contrasted fetchingly with the crisp white of her wedding dress. Her parents and Cane's parents had almost reached them. "I'll get you for that later," she threatened in a grim murmer.

Obviously Cane was totally without shame. "You certainly will!" he promised with prompt and indecent enthusiasm.

Recovering gamely, Brianna purred, "I do hope you're a man who intends to keep his promises," and for good measure, threw him a smile so full of sensual invitation that he groaned painfully from a sudden and acute attack of frustration.

Brianna turned to greet their families, a triumphant smile spread broadly across her face. *Have the last word, would he? Not if her name was Brianna Elizabeth Graeme Taylor!*

But Cane had the last word after all. While everyone was preparing to adjourn to the ranch where the mini-feast (as opposed to the maxi-feast of the upcoming barbecue) was waiting for them as part of the wedding celebrations, he announced smoothly, "Brianna and I are going to stop by the apartment before we come on out to the ranch. We want to change into something a bit more comfortable." He had already shed his suit coat and was tugging to ease the tight knot of his tie.

Exquisite courtesy forbade so much as the lifting of a skeptical or knowing eyebrow. Bland murmurs of agreement rose and fell around them like the soft susurrus of waves sliding against the shore. No one would ever be so crass as to intimate that Cane might be harboring a motive other than *comfort* when he announced the detour to the newlyweds' apartment!

Brianna was not crass. She was admiring. "Now that was what I would have to call a superb tactical maneuver," she congratulated him warmly while he steered the Blazer alertly through the stop-and-go town traffic. "I left some clothes out at the ranch, but I would *much* rather change at the apartment. How terrifically clever of you to arrange it so smoothly." She stretched across the center storage console—the Blazer was fitted with high-backed bucket seats—and ran an erotically explicit, exploratory hand from the bend of his right knee, lightly up the inside of his thigh.

The Blazer swerved ever so slightly. "If you're

not careful," Cane warned with a hoarse catch in his voice, "you'll get us 'arranged' right around the nearest light pole. Do you fancy to spend your wedding day in the emergency room of the hospital?"

"I thought you were a man who could do two things at once," Brianna teased, but she prudently removed her hand to a less provocative spot.

"I am doing two things at once," he announced as he applied the brakes and stopped for the fourth red light in a row. "I'm driving this vehicle and I'm also remembering exactly how you look stretched out on the bed without a stitch of clothes covering that lovely body of yours. Mortal man has his limits, you know," he informed her conversationally, "and sweetheart, when I'm thinking about you with no clothes on, believe me, I really only want to concentrate on doing one thing, and that *isn't* driving through crowded streets at the beginning of rush hour!"

Somehow, by drawing heavily on his deepest reserves of self-discipline, Cane managed to surmount each handicap—including aggravating traffic delays and his own rampant, randy imagination —to ensure that they arrived at the apartment unscathed . . . and without garnering a ticket for reckless driving. It was a praiseworthy accomplishment and Brianna was ready to reward him. As she watched him walk briskly, one might even say eagerly, around to her side of the Blazer, the hungry anticipation in her smile would have put a starving barracuda to shame . . . and she knew exactly where she was going to take the first bite! After all, if Cane was going to have to apologize anyway to each of their respective mothers for Brianna's and his tardy arrival, she might just as well make it worth his while!

They walked together, arms entwined, to the door of the apartment. After Cane had unlocked the front door and shoved it open, he lifted her easily into his arms and carried her across the threshold, into the familiar territory of his love.

Nine

After they finally arrived at the ranch, Cane made his and Brianna's apologies politely, if a trifle unconvincingly—mainly because he wasn't in the least sorry that they were late—and, as he had prophesied earlier to Brianna, neither mother was tactless enough to request an explanation for the newlyweds' tardiness. His dutiful apology was accepted with a bland good humor and any pointed remarks that came his way did so *sotto voce* from his brothers and his two partners, who were quick to take advantage of the liberties allowed by long friendship and blood relationship. Alex didn't comment—perhaps because Brianna was his *sister* —and Drew had had other priorities. To him, two less people present just meant two less mouths to contend for the guacamole and the other goodies his mother had spread for the feast. Drew had a very practical turn of mind when it came to food. After all, he was a growing boy!

The families seemed to be integrating comfortably, Brianna observed contentedly while she waited for her chance at a buffet table that her mother had loaded well past the groaning point. A relaxed atmosphere of camaraderie pervaded the gathering and, as far as she could judge, there wasn't a single lump of silent disharmony anywhere among the smooth mixture of cheerfully chattering people, all of whom seemed intent on celebrating a happy event at the top of their healthy lungs.

There was wine and there was song, and since she was now officially Cane's woman, Brianna had no complaints . . . except perhaps that her plate didn't seem to be big enough. She cautiously adjusted a succulent slice of honey-glazed ham in slippery equilibrium atop an unsteady pyramid of cherry jello and, for good measure, tucked in several pieces of stuffed celery wherever she thought there was room. Cane bent down and picked up the piece of celery that had landed, cheese side down, next to her foot. He tossed it into the nearest garbage can and then encouraged helpfully, "If you just pile the jello and the ham on top of your sourdough garlic bread, I'm sure that you can make room for another helping of potato salad and maybe some of those slices of fresh pineapple too." Deftly he caught another piece of celery as it tumbled off her overloaded plate, ate it with obvious relish and licked the cream cheese filling off the sides of his fingers.

Brianna shot him a disdainful look. "I'm hungry," she said with simple dignity. "Getting married is hard work. A girl has to keep her strength up."

"That's right," Jessica, Cane's younger sister, chimed in. She too was trying to fit the maximum food on the minimum plate. "Any woman knows that weddings are exhausting. That long walk down the aisle takes as much stamina as the Boston Marathon." She surveyed her tall brother scornfully. "All you men have to do is just stand there and wait for us to come to you. Why, it's no wonder that the man has to carry the woman over the threshold afterwards. The poor thing is so exhausted by her ordeal that she doesn't have enough strength left to step up over the sill."

"Ordeal?" Cane responded to his sister's teasing with confident amusement. "Oh, I hardly think that Brianna would characterize her marriage to me as an *ordeal*," he drawled with cool certainty. "Exhausting, perhaps," he continued irrepressibly, his intimate glance explicitly suggestive to both women. "And as for having strength . . ."

"Have some more celery, Cane darling," Brianna said sweetly and shoved a large piece heaped with a cream cheese and chopped green olive mix into his mouth with ruthless efficiency. Marriage—or something—was obviously having an outrageous effect on Cane's normally dry sense of humor. She only hoped that the effect wouldn't be permanent, otherwise she might, in the future, be forced to provide herself with a constant supply of mouth filling bites of food, because if Cane continued as he had begun, he'd be *fat* inside of a month!

While Cane crunched away manfully, Brianna said, "C'mon, Jess. Let's go find a quiet corner somewhere, where we can talk without interruptions. You can tell me everything that Cane doesn't want me to know."

"My life is an open book," Cane mumbled righteously around the celery.

"Don't talk with your mouth full, darling," Brianna admonished lightly. "I'm sure your life is an open book. I just want to make sure that none of the pages are stuck together." Sporting identical grins, the two women strolled away from him.

They dragged two chairs to the edge of the patio, set a small table up between them and sank onto the seats gratefully. After they had arranged their plates on the table, Jessica lifted her glass of champagne to Brianna in a silent toast, sipped and announced approvingly, "You've had an amazing effect on my brother, Bree. Quite astonishing, in fact. The whole family is agog."

"My family would say the same about Cane's effect on me," Brianna admitted with a soft laugh. She sipped from her own glass of champagne. "Even though they're used to my impulsive nature, my family is still reeling with shock at my sudden, unexpected dive into matrimony. You see, I've always been the original model for 'heart whole and fancy free,' but when I saw Cane"—she shrugged expressively—"well, that was that."

"It certainly was," Jessica agreed, with a delighted laugh, "and you must have hit him like the proverbial ton of bricks because, dear new sister, my brother Cane has never been the impulsive type. I love him dearly. He's my favorite brother and one of the nicest men I know, but I would have bet my pure silk teddy that when he fell in love, it would be calmly and rationally. It's the engineer in him," she explained. "Cane's mind moves clearly and logically from point A to point B, and from there inexorably on to point C, and he deals with the real world. If I had a problem, I'd go to Cane for help. He's affectionate and understanding, but impulsive? Never!" She grinned widely. "You'll be very good for him. Welcome to the Taylor family, Brianna."

"Thank you," Brianna accepted with demure mischief. "My family is equally approving of Cane. They're expecting him to be a stabilizing influence on me."

"Hmmm. I rather suspect that big brother will have his work cut out for him if that's the case," Jess assessed shrewdly. "I understand that you're a free-lance writer and that you travel quite a bit. Won't you find it hard to settle in one place permanently? It's really none of my business," she added hastily, "and you don't have to answer. It was just sheer curiosity."

"Oh, I don't mind," Brianna said with a small smile. "It's certainly a fair question, and heaven knows it's one that my family has already raised." She sighed. "Yes, I will find it hard to stay in one place for long periods of time. I'm the gypsy of the family and I wasn't ready to settle down. To be perfectly truthful, I don't know if I ever would have been," she admitted frankly, "if I hadn't met Cane. I won't quit writing, of course, but I will miss the traveling. I'll be working on a series based on my white water experiences next, after all the wedding excitement dies down and we get time to establish a reasonable routine."

"Are you and Cane going anywhere for a honeymoon?" Jessica asked curiously.

"No, not right away." This time Brianna's smile held an impish sense of mischief. "I'm afraid that Cane hasn't . . . er . . . been able to concentrate as fully as he should on the construction at the windfarm and now they're running a bit behind schedule. Besides," she added practically, "I just got back. I'd rather we take our honeymoon later, when it's more convenient for Cane and when," she added whimsically, but with a touch of sad truth, "the withdrawal pangs get more severe. Cane likes to backpack so maybe we can take a week or two off and go out to some wilderness area, or fly east and do a segment of the Appalachian Trail." Her eyes sparkled with anticipation. "I'd really enjoy that."

"You've really given this considerable thought," Jessica said, sounding slightly surprised.

Brianna laughed. "Of course. I may be impulsive, but I'm not actually scatterbrained. In reality, I'm a very practical person. I know exactly what I want, which is Cane, and I know what I have to do to keep him. It's all a matter of having your priorities straight," she concluded simply. "I've even got a possible idea for my next series, after I've finished the one on white water, and I can do all the necessary research for it right in the local area. See?" She tapped her forehead sagely. "Practical."

"Practical? Is some one accusing you of being practical?" Cane's voice was warm with amusement. He folded his long legs into a complicated tangle and sat down at Brianna's feet, leaning against her legs and balancing his plate in his lap. "Who could possibly have made such a baseless allegation? I thought everyone around here knew your reputation for leaping and not looking until after you're already airborne."

Brianna twitched slightly with a startled reaction that she was quick to mask, she hoped, by leaning forward to press her hand down on Cane's broad shoulder in a welcoming caress. She knew that they were finely attuned, but she hadn't suspected that he might be able to read her mind—at least, not on *other* subjects! Automatically, as though they moved independently of her conscious control, her slim fingers slid smoothly up the top line of his shoulder, slipping over the soft edge of his collar, down beneath his shirt to trace the firm hump of muscle at the side of his neck above the collar bone. When her seeking fingers moved lower, over the ridge of bone, down toward the muscled breadth of his chest, Cane sucked in a short, sharp breath and grabbed her hand, catching it beneath his shirt, arresting her further explorations. He slid his hand up over her wrist to her forearm and exerted slow leverage so that her arm was pulled across his chest, under his neck, drawing Brianna down so that she leaned forward, toward him. He tilted his head back and murmured a pleasant but firm warning, "If you keep that up, my sweet wife, not only will we have come rudely late to this celebration at which we are the guests of honor, but we will be leaving discourteously early." He released the pressure on her arm and smiled challengingly. "Carry on?" he invited hopefully.

With unmistakable reluctance, Brianna slowly tugged her hand out of Cane's light hold and, after trailing her hand lingeringly across the lean plane of his cheek, leaned back in her chair with a wistful sigh. "It's not nice to tempt Mother Nature," she remonstrated mildly, but her relaxation was mental as well as physical. It was clear that his jesting words had been accidental rather than deliberate, and she had mistakenly (she firmly rejected the word "guiltily") invested his casual phrasing with a significance he had not intended. She realized that Cane, even with the unique sensitivity of a lover, couldn't possibly have discerned the trend of her recent inspiration concerning a tentative theme for her next project. Why, she herself had just been infected with the exciting germ of the idea on Saturday while they were at the airport, waiting for the arrival of Cane's parents and younger brother, who were flying in together from Florida for the wedding.

She'd tell Cane about the idea—naturally she would!—when the time came, but right now the whole concept was still imperfectly formulated, still too vague, and she preferred to simply tuck the idea away into her subconscious to ripen. It had always been her custom to mentally incubate a possible idea for a new project until she had completely written up all aspects of the current project and she saw no reason to alter her established habit. There was certainly no hurry. After all, it wasn't as though she ever worked on a schedule, with a grimly looming deadline!

Besides—she gazed lovingly down at the top of Cane's head and stretched out a hand to stroke through the soft thickness of his hair—she had other, more urgently interesting things on her mind at the moment. She was going to freefall and she didn't need a plane to help her attain the heights. Cane would take her there!

Each hungry look Cane gave Brianna assured her that he was more than willing to "take" her anywhere she wanted to go, just as long as he could go right along with her. Unfortunately, good manners, as well as the knowledge that Cane's family had all traveled considerable distances to see him, meet her, and witness their wedding, precluded the newlyweds from deserting the celebration with indecent haste. They remained at the ranch, in the thick of the celebration, until other members of the party should show unmistakable signs of exhaustion. Yawns, however, are known to be highly contagious and Brianna, whose capacity for guile was enormous when the stakes were worthwhile, was guilty of subtly "seeding" the group she was in with an occasional ill-stifled yawn or two, just to get the ball rolling.

It could possibly have been attributed to Brianna's cunning use of psychological warfare or even ascribed to the fact that the amount of food consumed had gradually induced a condition of satiated stupor in most of the celebrants, or perhaps it was merely due to the simple realization that most of Cane's family had early morning flights to catch, but whatever the cause, the lucky effect—from Brianna and Cane's point of view— was that a general movement to speed the newlyweds on their way developed at a reasonable hour.

Prolonged goodbyes were exchanged—Cane and Brianna were *not* expected to escort the departing members of the family to the airport (Alex had graciously volunteered his services as chauffeur). Tentative plans for a reunion at holiday time were promoted, and finally Cane and Brianna were ready to depart.

Only one small incident marred their departure.

"Don't throw that rice at us!" Brianna ordered with a wail of horror. "It's a *fertility* symbol!"

Both mothers promptly grabbed double handfuls.

Brianna and Cane ran desperately for the shelter of the Blazer amid a veritable torrent of rice.

"Lord, I sure hope that Dr. Joe's pills work!" Brianna expressed a pious hope fervently while she shook the clinging grains out of her hair. "If they don't, your mother and mine have just insured that we'll have twins at the very least."

"I don't know about the possibility of twins," Cane commented grimly, "but I do know that we have a more immediate problem. Certain members of both of our families seem to have given full rein to their predictably low senses of humor, but I do think that they could have spared us the cowbells. The tin cans are bad enough."

They were out of sight of the lights of the ranch so he stopped the Blazer on the track, doused the lights and opened the driver's door. Brianna rummaged in the glove compartment and handed him the flashlight. Cane made a brief inspection at the rear of the car and reported disgustedly. "Do you have anything we can use to get this junk off the bumper? Even a nail file is better than nothing. I'll be damned if I'll drive through town trailing cowbells and tin cans and I didn't bring my pocket knife. My brother Daniel must have been in on this little stunt because the stuff is tied on with high-test monofilament line. That's what I used when I decorated his car when he and Kathy got married. I should have remembered that and been sure to pack a knife tonight."

"No problem," Brianna said calmly. She rummaged in the glove compartment again and pulled out a Swiss Army knife, bristling with blades. "I always keep this one in the car, as part of my emergency kit."

Cane made short work of the noisy decorations and tossed them into the Blazer in a clattering tangle behind the front seats. He climbed into the driver's seat and handed her the knife and flashlight. "I owe you an apology," he said ruefully as he started the engine and flicked on the headlights.

"Already?" Brianna feigned extreme shock. "We've been married less than twelve hours and you already owe me an apology?" She clucked sadly. "I don't know, Cane. That bodes ill for our hopes of marital happiness. Have we quarreled and I didn't notice?"

"Well, I was going to apologize for laughing at you when you told Jess that you were practical," Cane explained, "because the knife and the flashlight are certainly practical, but that also reminds me . . . I only caught part of the conversation. What new project did you have in mind?"

Brianna was blessed with an agile mind. "I'm going to research a how-to book," she said promptly. Her voice deepened and slowed to a seductive, throaty pitch. "A How-To-Drive-Your-Husband-Absolutely-Insane-With-Desire book. It'll be a long-term project and I'm afraid that it will necessitate extensive research. I've never done a book before, and of course the subject is new to me, but with the right research assistant, I'm positive I can come up with a first-class book. Would you happen to know of anyone who might be interested and qualified to help me with my research? I can guarantee excellent working conditions and full credit when the book is finished, even joint copyright. Unfortunately it will be a private printing, with an extremely limited distribution, but I think it would still be an attractive proposition for the right person."

"We should have brought the truck." Cane's husky voice seemed to be caught somewhere deep in his throat.

"Brought the truck?" Brianna repeated, bewildered by the *non sequitur*. "Why should we have brought the truck?"

"Because the truck has a bench seat," Cane said, "not a blasted center console like this Blazer. You're sitting too far away. If you were sitting next to me, I could start to convince you that I'm just the right man to help you with the research. In fact, if we had the truck and the truck had a mattress in the back, we could start on a chapter dealing with how to make your husband want to bay at the moon."

"I knew you were just the man I needed for a project like this," Brianna said with immense satisfaction.

That night they enthusiastically drafted the outlines for several basic chapters, beginning with "Why A Sexy Nightgown Is Wasted On Your Wedding Night" and including the useful and pertinent "How You Can Make Sure That Your Husband Will Wake Up With A Smile On His Face Even Though He's Only Had Three Hours Of Sleep The Night Before" plus the ever popular "A Breakfast In Bed With No Worry About Toast Crumbs."

In the week that followed they researched a chapter on "The Erotic Possibilities Of Massage" subtitled "Turn Over, Baby, And Let Me Do Something About Those Tight Muscles" and Brianna devoted considerable research time to a chapter entitled "How To Successfully Distract Your Man From The

Baseball Game He Was Watching On TV For Fun And Profit (Your Fun And Mutual Profit)."

In spite of their natural and wholly understandable preoccupation with the progress of the various chapters of the book, Cane and Brianna nevertheless established an efficient daily routine for that first week of marriage. After breakfast—with or without crumbs—at the apartment, they drove out to the ranch together where Cane concentrated on getting the construction of the windfarm back on schedule while Brianna helped her mother with the preparations for the big barbecue and, as a delightful bonus, got to know her mother-in-law much better.

Cane's parents had accepted the Graemes' warm invitation to extend their visit at the ranch, at least past the date of the party, when Cane and Brianna's marriage would be officially announced. David, Cane's younger brother, who had just graduated from college with a spanking new degree in computer engineering, was staying on too, but the other wedding guests, who had received the same hospitable invitation to stay longer, had regretfully declined and had departed to their various residences and responsibilities the day after the wedding.

Brianna wondered tiredly what part of her body was going to wear out first: her ear, her jaw or her hand. The phone at the ranch seemed to ring almost constantly and since fifty out of fifty callers were seeking confirmation of and information about the wedding, she had been protestingly but unanimously drafted to give the callers their information straight from the horse's mouth. Her pitiful whinnies of objection had been hard-heartedly ignored and when she wasn't talking on the phone, she was writing thank-you notes for the wedding presents that had started to pour in.

"I *knew* we should have just lived in sin," she grumbled darkly to Cane as she slumped exhaustedly against him while he drove the truck back toward their apartment the evening before the barbecue. "Nobody gives you presents when you shack up together and even if they're curious about your living arrangements, they generally don't discuss them to your face. Ohhh . . ." she moaned and tenderly massaged her jaw. "After tomorrow night I'm going to observe a vow of silence for one whole month!"

"Okay, just as long as it's not a vow of abstinence too," Cane acceded amiably.

"In case you hadn't noticed, I have just made a blatant bid for your sympathy," Brianna pointed out testily. "The least you could do is offer to help write some of the thank-you notes."

"False," Cane said cheerfully.

"False? What do you mean 'False'?" Brianna queried.

"I mean: False. The *least* I could do is *not* help you with the thank-you notes," Cane explained smugly. "Thank-you notes are women's work. I am a male chauvinist. I do not do windows or thank-you notes."

"Ha! I am a liberated woman. I do not do back massages or pick up dirty socks off the floor and drop them into the clothes hamper. Have we a basis for negotiation?"

"Sweet love, we have a basis for anything your little heart desires," Cane reminded her simply.

The words had been said as part of a jesting

exchange, but when Brianna remembered them several months later, she realized again that they were the light statement of a deep and enduring truth. She was out riding fence for her father in the back pastures, mounted on her mother's Appy mare, Angel Baby, Beelzebub's dam. The sweet-tempered, soft-mouthed mare had passed on nothing to her notorious son except her easy, reaching gait and the prized "blanket" markings. His temperament and his ears were his own.

As she urged the mare toward the crest of the nearest hill, following the line of the fence through the dry grass, Brianna's body swayed forward gracefully in an automatic adjustment to the mare's angle of ascent. When they reached the top of the hill, she reined in gently and took off her hat, shaking her curls free and lifting her face to the wind. She stood in her stirrups, stretched and then settled back against the cantle, kicking a foot free of the stirrup and hooking her leg comfortably over the pommel. The mare, sensing perhaps that they were going to be there for a while, stood quietly, head down, idly lipping the dry grass at her feet.

Brianna looked off into the distance, out over the rolling hills surrounding her, and breathed deeply of the hot, dust-tinged air. It was good—and necessary—to be out beneath the open sky and she flexed her shoulders unconsciously, as though temporarily shrugging out of a tight but invisible coat that chafed and constricted. She wished that Cane could have come with her to share this brief stretch of wings, but a crew was scheduled to pour concrete for more pads and he had to be there to supervise. She stared soberly down at the steeply angled line of the mare's neck and then out over the hills, but this time she was looking backward into time, not really seeing the golden vista.

Cane's parents had tottered gratefully onto the plane a day and a half after the barbecue—the party had gone on until six in the morning—and the bags under their eyes could have been checked through to their destination by the airline. David, with the recuperative powers of youth on his side, had fared a little better, but he too still showed the unmistakable effects of the rigors of celebration. Brianna and Cane had waved goodbye, watched the plane take off and then Cane summed it up nicely when he said, "My mother may decide to go back to the Everglades after all, just to rest up!"

Brianna, in turn, had voiced her own wry summation of her mother's magnum opus. "Our wedding didn't cost Daddy much, but the wedding announcement probably put the ranch in the red for a year! It'll take two trips in the truck to get all the beer kegs back to the distributor and we can start our own recycling center for glass, paper and aluminum."

It took several days after the party for everyone to clean up, rest up and catch up, but at last Brianna and Cane were able to settle into a comfortable and flexible routine. On the days that Cane worked at the site, Brianna would have breakfast with him at the apartment and later drive out to the ranch so that they could share the noon meal with the rest of the family. On those days, she always brought some contribution to the menu—a salad, a casserole or perhaps a thickly frosted cake—with her when she came and, after she had helped with the clean up, she usually went back to the apartment to do some writing.

Gradually she began to put together a satisfying series of articles based on her white water experiences. Their tone ranged all the way from the strictly factual to the downright whimsical, depending on her mood at the moment and the content of the particular experience she was remembering and recording. She was intrigued by the word processor capabilities of Cane's computer, but when it came right down to it, she found that she still preferred to pound out her articles on her old, battered but faithful portable typewriter. Cane frequently teased her about being an old-fashioned girl, using horse and buggy methods in a modern world, but she had her revenge when he lost a large chunk of current information during a brief and unexpected power outage. She smugly pointed out that *her* typewriter had better manners. It didn't eat up an article that she fed it and then sullenly refuse to disgorge it again!

It was an idyllic period of time. Marriage was a marvelous institution and Brianna would have unhesitatingly endorsed it to everyone. She was a happy woman. She had everything she needed, the creative outlet and stimulation of writing . . . and Cane.

Tongue in cheek, she had advanced the idea of a book whose subject was an exploration of the sensual pleasures possible when a man and a woman love each other, and when they possess both mutual desire and a generous, creative approach to making love. Although they'd never actually *write* the book, Cane and Brianna never wasted an opportunity for research. Waste not, want not . . .

And they met on levels other than the strictly physical. Jess had been right. Cane was intelligent, relentlessly logical and reality oriented. Without conceit, Brianna knew that her own intelligence was a match for his, but where Cane went from A to B to C on his way to D, Brianna was far more likely to go from A to D in one fell swoop and have no conscious idea of how she got there. It made for interesting discussions and sometimes no small amount of exasperation on Cane's part, expressed by his frequent cry of affronted logic: "But you *can't* get there from here!" when she had indisputably done just that! She also took a special mischievous pleasure in playing Devil's Advocate, that is, until Cane caught on to what she was doing and refused to rise to her bait anymore.

Every day and in every way, I love Cane more and more, Brianna paraphrased lightly but with absolute truth. Cane was essential to her. And yet . . . She sighed ruefully. He was *not* going to be pleased when she told him and *that* was why she was here, riding fence to the top of this hot, windy hill. She had finished the white water series of articles several weeks ago and had sent them all off on their appointed rounds. Now it was time to begin again and, no matter how she phrased it, she was afraid that her logical, rational, protective husband was not going to approve when she told him what she had chosen as the theme for her new series.

She had hoped that the familiar solitude and the peace of the open spaces would inspire her with some diplomatic method of presenting the concept to him. Unfortunately, all she had come up with so far was sweat. The mare shifted restlessly beneath her and Brianna curbed the horse automatically, soothing her with a brief pat and a comforting murmur. She lifted her hand to mop the moisture from her forehead with the back of her wrist and then froze in the classic pose of astonishment. Of course! What a blind idiot she had been. There it was, right in front of her nose, figuratively speaking. Actually, it was quite a few miles away and if she hadn't had good eyesight, she would have missed it completely, but the point was, she had just been visited by her hoped-for inspiration and she wasn't going to quibble about the finer details.

She slipped her foot back into the stirrup, waved a cheerful but unseen salute at the gaudy hot air balloon floating serenely many miles away, and reined the startled mare in a tight circle while she whooped happily with triumph and relief. Even though he didn't hear the wind sing, Cane wasn't *stodgy*. He'd had his share of adventures. Brianna knew that he was an experienced skin diver and that he liked to hike and to backpack into wilderness areas. He'd even done some caving, both dry land and underwater, an experience that Brianna had no particular desire to imitate. She wasn't exactly claustrophobic, not in the normal sense, but spelunking just didn't rate very highly on her private list of things she thought it might be fun to try. Anyway, the point was, Cane had shown that he did enjoy active pastimes. Now all she had to do was interest him in the particular activities that she wanted to incorporate into her newest project. How simple! Why hadn't she thought of it sooner? And she knew exactly which activity would be the perfect one to ... er ... "launch" her campaign. The mischief in her grin would have chilled the blood of *any* sober man.

She kneed the mare into motion, eager now to finish her task of checking the fence line. The sooner she got done, the sooner she could make some phone calls.

Ten

"Have we got anything special planned for this weekend?" Brianna asked casually while she served Cane a second helping of his favorite dessert, homemade strawberry shortcake with fresh whipped cream.

"No, not that I know of." Cane answered equally casually, a fine example of a satisfied and unsuspecting husband. "Why? Is there something in particular that you want to do?"

With an opening like that, Brianna couldn't miss, but she was much too wily a tactician to overplay her hand. "Well, I had thought that we might drive into San Francisco for the day. You haven't been to Chinatown or to the Embarcadero yet, have you?" she remarked in a most offhand manner.

Out of the corner of her eye, as she turned aside to set the whipped cream out of the way, she watched Cane mask a wince. One of the first things she had learned about her new husband was that he was not a particularly avid sightseer, although he did endure patiently whenever she expressed a strong desire to spend a day that way, just as she in turn good-humoredly attended the Country-Western concerts that he enjoyed at the Concord Pavilion. A marriage gained strength from those harmless compromises.

The snare was set.

"Or," she continued smoothly before he could comment, "we might go over to Livermore instead. There's going to be a hot air balloon exhibition there on Saturday and I thought it might be interesting to watch. Terry Coltrane knows a guy who owns a half-interest in one of the ones that's going to be part of the exhibition and she said that he'd be glad to let us ride along with him. She's gone up with him before and she loves it, says it's a marvelous experience."

Would he take the bait? She had presented it as attractively as she could contrive, but it would be fatal to seem overanxious. "Would you like your coffee now, darling?"

"Hmmm? Oh, no thanks," he declined abstractedly as he finished off the last bite of his dessert. "I'm too full for coffee. Dinner was delicious, sweetheart." He paused. "Which would you rather do?"

Gotcha! She pretended to consider the question for a moment and then said with nicely calculated enthusiasm, "Oh, the balloon ascent, of course. I've never been up in a balloon before and we can go sightseeing any old time."

"Okay, the balloon it is," he agreed indulgently. "Far be it from me to keep you from reducing by one your list of 'Things I Haven't Done Yet.'"

"But you'd like to do it too, wouldn't you?" Brianna asked anxiously. It was important that he really enjoy himself.

"Yes, you little schemer, I'll enjoy it," he admitted with a grin.

Brianna's eyes widened with shock. The only thing to do was bluff it out. "I am not a schemer," she denied indignantly, carefully following Mary Graeme's First Rule of Wifehood: Never Admit Nefarious Intent Even When He Catches You Redhanded.

"Oh, yes you are." Cane laughed. "Admit it. You really wanted to go up in the balloon all along. You never intended to drag me sightseeing on Saturday."

"You can't prove that." Brianna smiled triumphantly. "I can always take the Fifth."

His eyes narrowed with menace. "There are ways to make you talk," he assured her with silky intimidation. His glance down at her feet was heavy with ominous significance. "You see, my dear, your brothers have sold you out. They told me all about your Achilles heel . . . and your ticklish feet."

"You can't trust anybody these days," Brianna commented bitterly while she backed cautiously away from him. Cane rose slowly to his feet and shoved his chair out of the way. She took another step backwards and he took a slow step toward her. "A confession extracted under duress is worthless in a court of law," she reminded him desperately.

"Tell it to the judge," he instructed, poised to spring.

She spun on her toes, ready to run. He pounced.

"Aha! Gotcha!" He swept her up in his arms and surveyed his captive with what she privately characterized as distinctly pitiless intent. She decided to throw herself on the mercy of the court. She wound her arms around his neck and began to press lingering kisses on his bare throat.

"Can the judge be bribed?" she whispered.

"Certainly," he informed her promptly. "What did you have in mind to offer him?"

She murmured in his ear and a wide smile spread across his face. "Honey, with that kind of payoff, you can get away with murder in this court," the incorruptible magistrate promised instantly, and adjourned the court to the bedroom for immediate collection of his bribe.

At first it seemed as though Brianna's plan to reconcile Cane to the theme of her latest project was going to be successful. The balloon ascent was a masterstroke of strategy and an experience that they both enjoyed and were determined to repeat at the earliest opportunity. As instructed by Terry's friend, the pilot of the balloon, they arrived at the field at an hour Brianna mournfully described as being even earlier than the Dawn of Man. Cane promptly told her that it was far too early in the day to expect him to "weather" one of her puns and then went on immediately to explain with a suspiciously straight face that the reason that most balloon flights took place so early was to take advantage of the morning breezes and the atmospheric thermals. Because Brianna's thought processes were still slightly sluggish, it took a moment for Cane's more subtle verbal play to register, but when it did, belatedly, she dredged up the strength to cross her eyes and stick her

tongue out at him. This byplay earned her several
curious looks from the people standing near them,
but as the ground crews began to go to work,
Brianna's facial pecularities were forgotten.

Everyone watched with considerable interest—
and Brianna took copious mental notes—while
the crew rolled the balloon out of its bag and
stretched it out along the ground in a long roll.
While some members of the ground crew held the
balloon's mouth open, the propane burner was
moved into position and soon a bubble of heated
air began to writhe through the tough, multicol-
ored material that made up the bag until the
balloon filled, bulging majestically into its rotund
teardrop outline. With well-practiced efficiency and
care, the crew checked the rigging of the suspen-
sion ropes and helped the passengers clamber
into the basket. Restless, eager, the colorful craft
tugged impatiently at its moorings while the pilot
positioned the passengers for the proper balance
of the basket. Then, responding to the beckoning
caress of the breeze and accompanied by the soft
full roar of the propane burner, they lifted gently
into the air.

Other balloons rose before and after them, bright
variegated bubbles floating skyward, but Brianna
was only marginally aware of them. They went up
much faster than she had expected and she was
amazed at how quickly and smoothly the ground
fell away beneath them. Her eyes sparkled delightedly as they met Cane's and he saw for himself
the surging excitement that possessed her as she
savored the intoxication of the moment. He answered her smile, but his eyes were thoughtful.
He had seen that same expression on her face

before but only, he suddenly realized, as a pale reflection, when she had been talking about her river running experiences and, more vividly, when she *didn't* talk about them but seemed to be remembering some particular episodes that she wouldn't go into detail about. He was now visited by the uncomfortable suspicion that those episodes had been the really dangerous ones, the ones that she had never shared with her concerned family.

Of course, ballooning as a sport was not particularly dangerous in itself, barring accidents, but Cane began to wonder uneasily if his wild bird's wings had really ever been clipped or had her pinions merely been folded? He didn't doubt the continuing attraction of the lure he swung to call her. She would always respond to the lure of his love and its strength would summon her, bring her back to him, but how far away was she going to fly?

Brianna didn't have the faintest suspicion of the disturbing trend that Cane's uneasy speculations were taking. She was wholly engrossed in enjoying herself and her pleasure had an added dimension because she was sharing this marvelous experience with Cane. He was enjoying it too. She could tell. She smiled at him again, a smile that gleamed with the clear, uncomplicated radiance of a delighted child, whose every secret wish had just been granted.

It wasn't until later that Brianna realized that to Cane a balloon was one thing, but a parachute was something else entirely.

She hadn't been mistaken. Cane had enjoyed the balloon ride every bit as much as she had and he was perfectly agreeable, even enthusiastic, about going up again. He even suggested that she might consider doing some articles on the subject. They were sitting comfortably close on the couch after dinner, sipping wine, discussing the day's flight and their intention to accept the pilot's invitation to ride with him again.

Brianna slowly swallowed the last of her wine and cleared her throat. She hadn't intended to raise the subject just yet, but . . . She sighed. There wasn't any sense in putting it off any longer. She had the unhappy feeling that Cane wasn't going to take a favorable view of her plans no matter when or how she presented them to him.

"Well, now that you mention it," she began carefully, "I have had an idea for a new series of articles in the back of my mind for some time. You know that I finished the ones on river running some weeks ago, and this idea has been incubating until I was ready to start writing again."

"Just as a point of curiosity, did you already have this idea, whatever it is, in mind before we got married?" Cane asked quietly.

Brianna looked searchingly at him. His voice had been level, noncommittal, but there was something in his expression—his total *lack* of expression, to be precise—that was very odd. It was almost as though he was bracing himself to receive pain without flinching. "Sort of," she admitted honestly. "I mean, I got the germ of the idea while we were waiting at the airport for your parents and David to fly in before the wedding, but I didn't really start to refine it until I was nearly done with the last of the white water articles. I don't usually overlap my projects at all, but this one seemed like such a fantastic opportunity that I couldn't resist checking out a few things, just to see how well it was going to work. And darling, it's going to work beautifully." She allowed the enthusiasm to show in her voice. "It's going to be a lot of fun and I can hardly wait to get started."

"I see," Cane said heavily. "Why didn't you tell me before? Don't you think that this is something that we should have talked about a long time ago?"

Brianna flushed guiltily, but she met his eyes firmly. "I didn't mention it before now because I knew that you wouldn't approve," she admitted in a low voice, "and I didn't want us to argue about it until we had to."

"Because you knew that I wouldn't approve?" he repeated tensely. "Well, you were right! How the hell could I approve? I *don't* want you to be gone on some project for months at a time. I want you here with me. Damn it, Brianna, I love you! I want to be with you. You knew when we got married that I was going to be tied to the windfarm construction at your parents' ranch for at least a couple of years and maybe more if we start up other sites in the area. I can't go traveling with you all over the countryside for months at a time. You said that you understood, that you didn't mind waiting to take a belated honeymoon later on in the year. Well, let me tell you, Brianna Taylor, it'd be one hell of a poor honeymoon if only one of us goes on it!"

Brianna gaped at Cane with total amazement. "But . . . but I'm not going anywhere!" she blurted with a quick stammer. "Cane, I married you because I wanted to be with you, because I *have* to be with you. I love you. I wouldn't go away for even a night without you." Her voice dropped to a pained whisper and she looked at him out of penitent eyes. "I'm so sorry. I thought you understood that before."

"Oh, sweetheart," he groaned on a long shaken note and pulled her onto his lap, holding her so tightly that she thought her ribs really might crack this time. He pressed his face against the top of her head and she could feel the heat of his deep breaths spreading through the springy curls clustered over her head. He continued to hold her with a hard, desperate grip for a moment longer before his arms eased their hold fractionally, just enough so that she could breathe. "I had thought that I did understand before," he explained in a low voice, "but when I watched your face while we were up in that balloon this morning, I suddenly realized that maybe what I was demanding from you was something that you couldn't give. I've been selfish," he confessed. "I rushed you into marriage without giving you time to really think about what it all meant. Not just the loving, but the living together too. You had a career and a lifestyle that suited you perfectly and I just automatically expected you to reconstruct your whole way of living because I love you and because I asked you to marry me. The adjustments have all been made on your side, and I can't even offer to make any major ones on my side because I have prior commitments to my partners and your parents and the other investors that I have to honor.

"Anyway, when I watched your expression this morning while the balloon rose so lightly in the air, I knew that you'd been missing the old way of life, even though you hadn't said anything. I knew that I should be able to love you enough to let you come and go like your parents do, but I discovered that I can't love you unpossessively. I don't even want to try! Letting you go like they do would be like amputating half of my body. I'd start bleeding to death the minute you walked out the door."

"Oh, my dear love," Brianna said brokenly and lifted a quick hand to stroke away the pain shadows on his face. Cane, the logical, the rational, the engineer, had found words that she, who made her living from adjectives and flowing sentences, could not have expressed so beautifully had she polished and repolished the phrases 'til the typewriter ribbon wore all the way through. Could she do as well by him in her turn? Because it was her turn now. Lies, even a lie by omission, had no place in their relationship. Cane had already been hurt by a misinterpretation. It was time for her to speak plainly.

Cane scanned her troubled face intently. He drew in a deep slow breath. "There's something else, though, isn't there, sweetheart?" he asked gravely. She could feel the tension creep back into the long line of his body. "You aren't planning to leave me and travel alone," he added, "but there's still something I don't know, something you haven't wanted to tell me because you knew that I wouldn't approve." His smile twisted awry. "You even said as much just before I got onto the wrong track." His brow furrowed in concentration.

He had just left A on his way to B, but Brianna wanted him to get to C by a route she chose so she laid a soft finger on his lips and said, "Hush. I'll explain, but first there are some things you have to understand. The first is, yes, I do miss being able to travel where and when I will. I liked that freedom. If I had never met you, I would probably still be traveling that way even when I became a white-haired little old lady in a motorized wheelchair. But"—she pressed her finger more firmly against his lips when he would have spoken—"*but* I gave it up of my own free will. I saw you, I loved you at once and, contrary to what you firmly but erroneously believe about me, I am a *very* practical person. I knew at once that I couldn't have both you and my old freedom. Something had to go and it wasn't going to be *you!*

"Now," she continued with a slight smile, "I will admit that we did rush into marriage. Notice, please, that I said 'we' because I was there too. It was a mutual rush, not a unilateral one, and I do deny that I came into this marriage without giving it considerable thought. I know that you think that my mind moves in mysterious ways and wonder that it performs at all. . . ." He winced and muttered "Incorrigible!" with a rueful shake of his head, but he smiled when he said it, and she continued, "But it arrived at exactly the same conclusion that yours did. You couldn't travel with me, so . . ." she drawled, "I will stay with you, and that"—she lifted her hand from his mouth and dusted her hands together in a dismissive gesture—"takes care of that."

And now, she was very much afraid, came the tricky part.

"That takes care of my lifestyle, BC and AC, but now we come to the second point, my career," she said steadily.

"Whoa," Cane interrupted. "BC and AC?"

"Before Cane and . . ."

"After Cane," he finished. "Naturally. Sorry to
be so dense." Then his eyes narrowed in realization. Cane had just arrived at "C," before Brianna
really wanted him to, and it didn't look as though
he liked what he had found once he got there.
"Dense. That's a fair description, all right," he
accused himself disgustedly. "Brianna," he said
carefully, "I know that you aren't going to stop
writing, nor do I want you to because you are a
very talented lady, but *what* are you going to
write about?"

He had a way of going right to the heart of the
matter, Brianna admitted wryly, with reluctant
admiration. It was that relentlessly logical mind.

"I'm going to write about ballooning," she admitted cautiously.

She inspected the fingernails on her left hand
meticulously, waiting for a reaction, any reaction,
from him. There wasn't any. She risked a glance
over at him and found him staring right back at
her. Waiting. Impassively. There was a rather grim
set to his jaw that she mistrusted instinctively.
There were advantages and disadvantages to sitting on his lap when she told him what else she
was going to write about. She considered them
briefly. She wondered if it would appear suspicious if she got up from his lap and strolled casually around the room? She shifted experimentally
and his arms tightened around her waist ever so
slightly. *"Oh well,"* she thought philosophically,
*"a coward dies a thousand deaths, et cetera, et
cetera. . . ."*

"I'm going to do a series about . . . er . . . activities that are . . . er . . . flight related." She coughed

slightly and cleared her throat and wished that she hadn't already drunk all of her wine.

"Got a feather in your throat?" Cane asked, but his voice was as grim as the set of his jaw. "Have some of my wine." He bent forward and picked up his glass from the floor, crushing Brianna slightly in the process, but he didn't ease his hold on her at all. He handed her the glass, waited while she drained it—there really wasn't much left anyway—and then set it back in the same spot on the floor, mashing her again in passing. She glared at him and thought she detected the faintest subterranean twinkle, but she couldn't be sure. That jaw still had a hard, sharp line to the bone. No twinkle could stand up to it.

Cane waited.

"I'm going to learn to fly a plane. And a hang glider. And I'm going to learn to free fall. I've signed up for the lessons and I start ground school next Wednesday. We learn to pack our own parachutes," she finished in a breathless rush and her own jaw thrust out defiantly.

There was a long silence while Cane sat as though turned to stone. Brianna sat rigidly upright in the loose circle of his arms, waiting. Finally she felt his chest expand in a deep, silent sigh. "I don't suppose it would do me any good to ask you to forget the hang gliding and the skydiving, would it?" he asked quietly. His face was pale under its tan and his eyes were expressionless, a bleak washed-out blue.

She looked steadily at him, her own eyes glassily bright. "Please don't ask me," she whispered. "Please, Cane, don't ask me."

That night they made love with an urgency in

their passion that approached ferocity and desperation and by the next morning a tacit truce was in effect. They avoided the subject of Brianna's writing completely. It was no solution, but it was a way to live with the problem, at least for a while.

Brianna honestly didn't know what she would have done had Cane pressed his plea—for plea it had been—for her not to participate in the two sports that he felt were too dangerous. She might well have acceded to his request, made in the name of love, but what would it have done to their relationship? And what would it have done to it if he had made the request and she had refused? Thank God he had not pressed the issue!

Cane knew why he hadn't pressed the issue and every day that she went out to the airfield for the sky-diving lessons he paid the grim cost of his decision. He, like Brianna, had been afraid of the damage that would be done to their relationship, no matter which answers he gave, had he insisted on asking the question. He was wise enough to know that to confine a wild bird forcibly is to run the risk of destroying it, and even if it survives its confinement, what is left will be a poor pathetic wraith of the once proud spirit.

He was a patient man. She had chosen to stay with him, chosen freely to give up that wider range that she had once flown at will, all that she might sleep by his side and in his arms each night. He would not risk the loss of what he had already and he would hope for much more, also freely given. In the meantime, he could only shield his heart and mask his expression each time she walked out the door.

"We're jumping today."

Cane carefully finished buttering his toast and then meticulously spread the red raspberry preserves thickly over the bread from edge to edge. He concentrated on his task and didn't look up at her. "What time?" It was a simple question, devoid of all emotional content.

"I have to be there by nine, but I don't think we're scheduled to jump until sometime after eleven, so I probably won't be home for lunch," Brianna said carefully. "I can leave you a cold lunch, if you'd like, or if you're going to be out at the site, I can call Mom and tell her to expect you for lunch with them."

"No," he declined, "I'm going out there first thing this morning, but then I have to come back into town so I'll either get a hamburger someplace or come back here and fix myself something. Don't worry about me." His voice was matter-of-fact. He began to eat his toast.

There hadn't been the slightest tinge of irony or emphasis in Cane's voice when he had spoken those last four words, but Brianna looked at him with troubled eyes. The lines of his face were subtly thinned by a slight draw of tension that she had come to recognize, and his eyes were hooded and somber, as they always were whenever she made that brief announcement at breakfast time.

She had been jumping now for a month, but they didn't talk about it very much. Cane had never tried to dissuade her, but he would neither participate nor come to watch her. The only mention of that particular activity of hers came simply with each brief announcement and the fact that now and again she missed lunch with him. She had noticed too that her family didn't ask about the sky diving either, although they were warmly interested in the ballooning that she and Cane had both continued to enjoy, so much so that they were considering the possibility of buying a small interest in the balloon that they had taken their first ride in. She sighed soundlessly. She had hoped that he would eventually become reconciled but he hadn't. Obviously.

Cane was on his way to the apartment when the news bulletin came crisply over the truck's radio, a "teaser" with the promise of more details on the hourly news report. A plane had just crashed at the airport. Details as yet were sketchy, but it was believed that a plane full of sky divers had crashed upon takeoff and exploded. There was no word on survivors, if any.

He drove immediately to the airport, suspended all the while in an anesthetic fog of numb disbelief, and reached a scene of nightmare. Greasy black smoke still curled in evil tendrils from the wreckage while ambulances waited with somber patience off to the side. When he saw two firemen begin to spread long sacks of heavy dark plastic in a tidy, tragic row, ready to receive their grim burdens, the gorge rose in his throat and he swallowed furiously.

With numb persistence he went from group to group until finally he found the head of the jump school.

"I was told that there were two planes going up today and that the other plane took off safely," Cane said hoarsely. "Who is in that other plane?"

Tears had streaked a dirty track through the

smoke grime coating the other man's face and he said wearily, "I don't know."

Cane grabbed him by the shoulders and said fiercely, "For God's sake, man, you've *got* to know! My wife was going to jump today. She could be in that . . ." He couldn't complete the sentence. He shivered convulsively and swallowed desperately as they looked toward the blackened, twisted hulk that the firemen were now approaching cautiously.

"I tell you, I *don't* know!" the jump school manager insisted. "I don't know who went on what plane. I don't have a list. We won't know until the other plane gets back. We called it back from the drop zone and it should be here in a few minutes." His voice cracked in a choked whisper. "The only one I know for sure was on that plane"—his hand moved in a small painful gesture—"was my best friend. He was the pilot." He turned away and hunched his shoulders.

Not allowing himself to think, not allowing himself to believe one way or the other, Cane stood alone, waiting for the second plane to come back. When he heard the drone of its engines approaching, he seemed to shrink briefly, drawing into himself, shoulders rounding and body bracing to accept an unendurable pain. As the plane landed and taxied toward the parking apron, carefully skirting the ravaged skeleton of its sister plane, he straightened slowly, moving toward the place it would park like a very old, very tired man until he stopped and stiffened, standing erect, shoulders pulled back and braced, ready to receive his sentence of life . . . or death.

The plane stopped, the engines' roar chopped off abruptly, and after a long pause, the door in its side opened with agonizing slowness. Several people jumped out and one landed awkwardly, stumbling and going down to one knee, but Cane ignored them. They were not the one he had to see. His hands clenched unconsciously at his sides and the muscles in his jaw stood out in graven relief. A black, curly head appeared in the doorway of the plane, downbent as she watched her footing. A low, inarticulate moan was pulled from his parted lips with the harsh exhalation of the breath he had been holding.

Brianna stepped carefully down from the plane. The person who had climbed out before her had fallen and she didn't want to follow him. They were all shocked and shaken and her legs felt curiously rubbery. They hadn't known anything about the crash before their pilot had curtly announced that the jump was canceled and they were returning to the airport. When pressed he could only say that there had been an accident, but the tragic extent of the disaster had become evident to all while they had circled before landing.

She started to walk away from the plane, still carefully watching where she put her feet because that way she didn't have to look over toward the stomach-turning, crumpled wreck. A sudden compulsion made her lift her head. Cane stood like a statue twenty feet away, watching her, his hands hanging limply at his sides, palms out, fingers loosely curled. She could see the tears running unheeded down his face and his eyes held such a mixture of indescribable joy and unendurable pain that she felt the tears sting, then overflow her own eyes. She walked into his arms and he pulled her against his shaking body with a gesture that was as strong as love, as poignantly expressive as any strangled groan of anguish. He rocked slowly, murmuring her name over and over in a broken husky voice, and she cried in his arms for his pain, because it was her pain too. He had died in slow, infinitely prolonged agony each minute that he had endured while waiting for her to step out—or not step out—of the plane. Now she suffered his return to life with him, not because he said anything other than that broken repetition of her name, but because she experienced through him what she would have suffered had the positions been reversed, had she been the one to stand waiting, not knowing.

She didn't know how long they stood there, locked together in reunion, but finally Cane eased his desperate clutch of her and said hoarsely, "Let's go home."

They took the truck and Cane drove slowly and carefully, his face gray-tinged with exhaustion. Brianna sat as close to him as was humanly possible without actually climbing into his lap, her hand curved over the muscle of his thigh, her head leaning against his shoulder. They hadn't broken physical contact from the moment she had walked into his arms, holding hands even while she climbed into the truck. They desperately needed the affirmation that the continued physical contact provided.

When they reached the apartment, Brianna headed toward the bedroom, but Cane pulled her to a halt by the telephone. "Not yet." He gestured toward the phone with his free hand. "Call your parents. They might have heard about the crash and be worried." His words held the echo of his own recent pain.

It was fortunate they did call because Alex was just on the point of driving into town to try and get information. Mary had heard the news report. Her frantic calls to the apartment had naturally gone unanswered and her calls to the airport had been of little greater value. Now, reassured, she extracted a promise that Cane and Brianna would come out to the ranch for dinner and then let them go with heartfelt words of thankfulness for Brianna's safety.

"*Now,*" Cane said huskily as he directed her toward their bedroom. He needed to affirm her existence in the most basic way possible.

They had made love many times before, and would do so many times again, but this time became a slow, sweet celebration of life that Brianna would remember all of her days. Cane undressed her slowly, touching every part of her body with gentle reverence, as though reassuring himself that she truly stood whole and unhurt before him. When he knelt beside her on the bed as she lay waiting for him, she could trace every raw emotion that he had experienced during the day in the stark lines scoring his face. She knew then what she wanted to tell him before they made love. There must be no shadow of future fear to shade their union.

Before his hands could move to her body, she captured them and clasped them against her breast. "My dear love, I've come home now. I won't go away again." He looked at her with uncomprehending eyes and she said clearly, "You won't have to ask me not to do foolishly dangerous things, Cane. Not any more. I love you. You're the most important thing in my life and today I almost lost our future together. Nothing means more to me than that and I'm telling you now that I admit it with my mind as well as my heart. I want to live to be a very old lady, just as long as you're right beside me as a very old man, and there's no sport or activity that's worth the deliberate risk of those lovely years."

Her voice held quiet resolution and her smile a serene radiance. "I'll write about many things, but they'll be things we've done together." Her hands released his and began to move on his body, pulling him down to her. "We might even work on a book together," she murmured invitingly.

Cane came willingly down to her, his slow smile matching hers for bright radiance. All he had ever wanted was held in his arms. His wild bird had been caught and tamed by love.

THE EDITOR'S CORNER

Our LOVESWEPT romance publishing program increases from three to four titles every month with our February list. We hope you'll feel that each of our love stories next month is a special Valentine's Day present—long-stemmed, exquisite yellow roses from Iris Johansen; a delectable selection of bon-bons from Kay Hooper; a warmly satisfying vintage wine from Dorothy Garlock; a bottle of haunting and evocative perfume from Fayrene Preston.

THE GOLDEN VALKYRIE, #31, is another dramatic and fast-paced love story from Iris Johansen whose works you've written such glowing letters about since we introduced her last August. In this gripping, yet often highly amusing tale, the "golden valkyrie" is the large, but very lovely private detective Honey Winston. The hero is a much publicized member of royalty known as "Lusty Lance." And the episode that brings these two characters together is as surprising as it is delightful. But Honey quickly sees the real man and the sensitive artist behind the gossip column image of the outrageously attractive Prince Rubinoff. And, armed with insights and a tender commitment to him, she sets out to free him from his gilded, but limited existence. This is a passionate and truly exciting story.

C.J.'S FATE, #32, is witty and wonderful . . . another of those delicious confections we've come to expect Kay Hooper to whip up for us. We at Bantam are delighted to welcome Kay as a LOVESWEPT author and to present this romance as her first—but certainly not her only—LOVESWEPT. We think you'll

(continued)

laugh out loud throughout this charming story of an unsuspecting woman who discovers romance when and where she least expects it; you'll sigh a lot, too, over the winsome tenderness of Kay's dashing hero—and his efforts to woo his lovely lady. Right along with C.J. you'll keep falling harder and harder for the wise, funny, and deeply romantic lawyer who plays havoc with her emotions!

THE PLANTING SEASON #33, is another of the heartwarming, believable romances for which Dorothy Garlock is known and loved by a legion of devoted fans. Set on a working farm, **THE PLANTING SEASON** is uniquely American, a harvest of touching emotion for the reader. Dorothy's heroine, Iris Ouverson, is a mature woman, experienced in dealing with the vagaries of the elements, yet innocent about romance. Against her will, Iris is forced to share the land she loves with a stranger, John Lang, who knows nothing of the hardships of wrenching a living from the earth, yet seems to know too much about how to sweep a woman off her feet. As touching as Dorothy's first LOVESWEPT (#6, **A LOVE FOR ALL TIME**), **THE PLANTING SEASON** is a romance you won't want to miss!

In LOVESWEPT #21, **THE SEDUCTION OF JASON**, published last October, Fayrene Preston introduced a secondary character—the kooky, absolutely unique, and very touching Samuelina Adkinson. "Sami," as she's known to her friends (and oh what a large and varied group that is!), now has her own romance: **FOR THE LOVE OF SAMI**, #34. Daniel Parker-St. James is the sort of hero around whom romantic fantasies must be woven—a man who is tender, considerate, passionate, powerful. And all the promise that Fayrene, demonstrated in her three previous works is fulfilled magnificently in this vibrant, extraordinary love story!

Roses ... Candy ... Rare wine ... Haunting perfume—the "gifts" of the four LOVESWEPTS for Valentine's Day. And they aren't fattening or intoxicating and they certainly aren't perishable! In fact, we hope you enjoy each LOVESWEPT so much that you will keep it to enjoy again and again as time goes by. With warm good wishes,

Carolyn Nichols

Carolyn Nichols
   Editor
LOVESWEPT
Bantam Books, Inc.
666 Fifth Avenue
New York, NY 10103

Love Stories you'll never forget
by authors you'll always remember

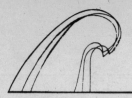

*Love Stories you'll never forget
by authors you'll always remember*

☐	21630	**LIGHTNING THAT LINGERS #25** Sharon & Tom Curtis	$1.95
☐	21631	**ONCE IN A BLUE MOON #26** Billie J. Green	$1.95
☐	21632	**THE BRONZED HAWK #27** Iris Johansen	$1.95
☐	21637	**LOVE, CATCH A WILD BIRD #28** Anne Reisser	$1.95
☐	21626	**THE LADY AND THE UNICORN #29** Iris Johansen	$1.95
☐	21628	**WINNER TAKE ALL #30** Nancy Holder	$1.95

Prices and availability subject to change without notice.

Buy them at your local bookstore or use this handy coupon for ordering:

Bantam Books, Inc., Dept. SW, 414 East Golf Road, Des Plaines, Ill. 60016

Please send me the books I have checked above. I am enclosing $_____
(please add $1.25 to cover postage and handling). Send check or money order
—no cash or C.O.D.'s please.

Mr/Mrs/Miss _____

Address_____

City_____ State/Zip_____

SW2—1/84

Please allow four to six weeks for delivery. This offer expires 7/84.